Lust & Found

Ann Moran

Ann Moran

Dedication

To WAM—The man, not the law firm

Acknowledgement

Thanks to Bill, Gary and Joan for their helpful comments. And a special thank you to my buddy, Bill, for suggesting I tweak the title.

Chapter One

I smile when I see the name of the Sender on a message sent to my Kaity Kinney email address and open the email:

Please contact me.

The Sender is Matt Dwyer, and his telephone number follows his message. Matt's a friend I've not had contact with for many years, and I flash back to another place in time.

We met almost twenty-five years ago when we were in our teens, both of us working after-school jobs at the same Chicago grocery store. We became friends and on nights we were both working, Matt walked me home after work.

I was attracted to him and felt a stirring deep within me the first time we met. My heart raced, and I wondered what it would be like to be in his arms and to feel his lips on mine. I also wondered what it would be like to do some other things as well. But except for our friendship, Matt didn't show the slightest bit of interest in me, and I couldn't guess why—or perhaps more precisely, why *not*?

I wonder if Matt knows I'm back in Chicago, although he probably isn't even aware I left the city when I had what surely had been an early midlife crisis six years ago. I also wonder if he knows my first marriage to his former Little League buddy didn't last. I'm doing a lot of wondering—and continue to do so—as I wonder if my current lack of male companionship is the reason Matt's email seems to be having more of a profound effect on me than it should.

I call him and hold my breath while I wait for him to answer his phone. And then I hear his voice. "Matt Dwyer."

I allow myself to breathe. "Hi Matt, it's Kaity Kinney."

"Kaity! It's so good to hear from you! I called you when I heard you returned to Chicago."

So, he does know about my midlife crisis.

I returned to the Windy City after divorcing my second husband, whom I met online and then moved to San Francisco to be with him on a whim. The very thought sends a chill through me, and I shiver. We divorced because I could no longer stay in an abusive marriage, but to the rest of the world I pretended it was because he was still in love with his ex-wife. The latter didn't reflect on my stupidity or cowardice for why I stayed in the marriage for as long as I had.

I'm still humiliated. And added to my mortification is the unhappy fact that my two failed marriages make me a two-time loser. The good news is that I finally had the good sense to come home, and I've been back in Chicago for almost two years. And it's my good fortune that I was able to return to my position as a paralegal at the law firm where I was employed before I foolishly rushed off to San Francisco. Working at a place I love, along with the people I work with, helped me get my head back on straight.

"I called several times," Matt says. He laughs and adds, "I suppose I should have left messages."

Hearing his voice gives me a boost I didn't know I needed, and I laugh with him. "Messages would have been helpful, so I'd have known to call you back."

"Are you still working at WAM?" he asks.

WAM is Williams, Anderson & Mason. I began working as a secretary at the law firm after high school graduation and later went on to get my paralegal certificate. "Yes, and I love my job. We're getting ready to go to trial in Boston next month."

I'm working from home in preparation for the upcoming trial, writing case summaries and doing research for Zach Eberle, the litigation partner I'm assisting. Zach and I have known each other for years, and we work well together.

"I remember you enjoyed law firm life," Matt says, "so good for you."

I do enjoy law firm life. I work hard, and proof of my hard work surrounds me. Printouts of court cases, along with the legal pads holding my notes, are strewn across my kitchen table and countertops because the desk in my home office is cluttered with the paperwork generated by my research.

I also enjoy talking with Matt and, at the moment, he's, my priority. "Enough about me. Tell me about you."

"I was a firefighter/paramedic until I was injured during a call several years ago. The injury prevented me from continuing to fight fires, and I was required to take an early retirement. I work the insurance business that once had been my side job, and I own some property that needs looking after. I spend any spare time I have helping friends with various repair projects."

"I heard you married Vera Cozzi," I say.

"You heard right, but we divorced more than a year ago. After seventeen years of marriage, she suddenly decided we should go our separate ways."

Seventeen years is a long time, so that had to hurt. "Sorry to hear that, Matt. It must have been awful not to have had any warning."

"I should have seen it coming. We'd been drifting apart for years, so I wasn't disappointed."

It hurts my pride more than my heart, but we touch on my failed marriages as well. Matt heard about both of them, so I don't go into detail except to say, "Your old baseball buddy decided he wanted to play the field, but it wasn't on your old baseball field that he wanted to play."

"I'm sorry, Kaity, but I'm not surprised. My surprise was that you stuck with him as long as you did."

"Did you know?"

"I heard the scuttlebutt," he admits. "He didn't deserve you, and I think you knew that was my opinion back when we were working together. What happened in San Francisco?"

I shiver again. I lost my mind. That's what happened. I don't know how to explain my foolishness, and it's impossible to justify why I stayed so long in what initially seemed to be a promising relationship that went from bad to worse. I'm still trying to put it behind me and nowhere near ready to talk about it. "Let's save that conversation for another day."

Matt kept up with some of our old friends, and he updates me with what he knows of the happenings in their lives. "Bonnie moved to Reno, and Otto went in the other direction. He's now living somewhere in New Hampshire. Sue and Vince are still happily married, and they now have a couple of kids. Remember the lovebirds?"

"Kelly and Mark. I remember when they got engaged. They were crazy about each other."

"Well, Kelly didn't marry Mark," Matt says and laughs. "She married his brother instead!"

"That's too funny," I say and laugh with him.

When our laughter subsides, I say, "I'm living just outside the city now. Are you still living in Chicago?"

"No, I moved to Pocah County, where I've gotten very involved with my community."

Despite the many filings I've made on behalf of the law firm, I never filed anything for any court in Pocah County. I've never even heard of Pocah County. "Where is Pocah County?"

"It's a small county located near Peoria, about a hundred fifty miles southwest of Chicago, and I was recently recruited to run for office in my township."

"Way to go, Matt!"

"Thanks. I'm still playing baseball twice a week, so I'm in the city quite frequently. The next time I'm downtown, how about if I take you to lunch?"

I'm still my five-foot-two petite self with eyes a deep shade of green, but is Matt still thinking of me as the sixteen-year-old girl he was friends with? Since we're both on the wrong side of forty now, and time has begun to take its toll, I don't want Matt to be disappointed that the sixteen-year-old girl he remembers is not sweet sixteen anymore. But the real issue is that I haven't been downtown in weeks. "Thanks for the invite, Matt, but I'm mostly working from home these days."

"That sounds like a nice arrangement," he says.

It's a great arrangement. Being able to work from home makes life so much easier without having to commute to and from downtown Chicago every day. Another perk that comes with working from home is that the dress code is jeans and T-shirts, and bras are optional. "It's a very nice arrangement," I say.

"You must have a terrific boss."

"I do. My boss is the best." And although Zach has given me a new time-consuming research assignment, working from home also means I can still find time to talk, text and email with Matt.

"So, you're going to Boston next month," Matt says. "Preparing for trial must keep you busy."

"The prep work does keep me busy. With all you do, I'm guessing you're also keeping busy."

"Very busy," he says. "I'm often overwhelmed with all I have to do. I've been meeting with my political cohorts and doing some campaigning, and I don't have time for much of anything else these days."

He's working his insurance business and taking care of his property. He's involved with his community and running for office in his township. And he's still playing baseball and helping friends with repair projects. Matt seems to have the energy of a ten-year-old boy.

While I contemplate his energy level, his voice turns serious. "You changed my life by the simple act of befriending me, Kaity, and for that I will be forever grateful. It's important to me that you know that."

I'm so surprised that I'm unable to find my voice.

"I never looked at you in the light of attraction because you had a boyfriend. Although I didn't think he deserved you, I didn't feel it was my place to say so."

I had lots of boyfriends, as did most teenage girls, but that might explain Matt's long-ago disinterest in me.

"Also, I never thought someone as pretty as you would consider having me in your life, so I felt blessed that you let me walk you home after work."

My surprise morphs into astonishment, and I still cannot reply.

"But what you did for me. You opened the door for me to finally become part of a neighborhood and to have friends and activities to participate in with my new friends. You gave me the 'extended family' I needed in my life."

Something surges through my chest, and my heart does a cartwheel.

~ * ~

We have another telephone conversation the following day that lasts for hours. Matt's as easy to talk to as I remember, and I pace my kitchen while we reminisce. There's so much to talk about, and I remember his red hair, his boyish smile and his easy laugh. And his hands. I remember his large hands and long fingers and feel myself blush. My heart skips a beat, and I wonder if something might be happening between us after all these years.

Matt and I talk, email and text over the next few days, and I still have so much more I want to share with him, and so many more questions I want to ask.

He writes in an email:

What I would like you to know, as I reflect back on when we first met, is the gift you bestowed upon me. You have no idea how you changed my life, Kaity, and I pray for the moment that I can share with you how your influence has helped to shape me. I believe you'll be proud, not only of me but of yourself as well, when you learn to what you contributed.

Because of what I have lived through in my life and what I have witnessed in my years as a firefighter/paramedic, I like to sign off with the last words I want my friends to hear from me, and those words are "Sending love."

A sense of something joyful touches my heart after reading Matt's email.

He calls later that day, and I tell him, "You're spoiling me with your emails."

"If I thought there'd been an opening for me back in the day, I'd have spoiled you for the rest of your life."

His words turn my skin to gooseflesh, and my heart does a backflip. I wonder again if something might be happening between us.

We have to end the call, though, because Matt's driving in a remote area and keeps losing his cellphone signal. He says he'll call when he has better reception.

Matt doesn't call before bedtime, and I go to sleep missing him. I remember again his large hands and long fingers and hope I dream of him.

~ * ~

I'm asleep in my bed when dream Matt crawls in to lie beside me.

His dream kiss wakes me up. "Hello, Sleeping Beauty," he says, and kisses me again, this time with tongue. He lifts my nightgown, then caresses my breasts and sucks my nipples.

My wet immediately begins to flow, and I tell him, "It's been a long time for me."

"No worries, Kaity, I'll be gentle." He's naked, and he takes my hand and places it on his dick. "Stroke me," he tells me, and I do.

He removes my panties and inserts a long finger into my opening. My wet flows over his finger and my breath catches in my throat. When he's fully erect, he moves above me and enters me slowly, pushing gently until his dick is all the way inside me. He withdraws and enters me again, thrusting and then plunging his very large, very hard cock into me.

He pushes and pounds, and I move my hips to push and pound with him. I'm on fire! An incredibly powerful orgasm rushes through my body at the same time dream Matt shudders and ejaculates into me.

"I'd like it if you would come to bed naked. No nightgown and no panties," he tells me.

And then dream Matt is gone.

~ * ~

I sit up in bed. Holey Moley. I'm alone and shivering, and the bedsheet is damp. I move to the other side of my bed and go back to sleep. Dreaming of Matt.

Chapter Two

I awaken the next morning, and my breath catches in my throat when I remember Matt holding me in my dream, our bodies joined, and I feel myself shudder.

I'm anxious to check my email to see if he's written, and I'm disappointed that he hasn't. I continue working on my research project, but continuously check my email.

When I still haven't heard from him by noon, I call him. The call goes straight to voicemail, so I text him instead:

You didn't call back last night or send an email this morning.
I hope I haven't scared you away.

I get immersed in my work after I send the text and lose track of time. When I take a dinner break several hours later, I realize I still haven't heard from Matt. I put together a salad and go back to work after eating. It's late when I finally turn off my computer, and there's still no word from Matt.

I go to bed praying he's okay and hope the reason he hasn't called is because of bad cellphone reception and not because he's lost interest in reconnecting with me. And I hope I'll dream of him again.

~ * ~

I get up several times during the night to check my phone for a text or an email to no avail. Each time I go back to sleep, I dream of Matt. I check my phone again when morning rolls around. Still nothing from Matt.

I'm back to work on my research assignment, but I have a difficult time concentrating. It's almost noon when Matt finally calls.

"Good day, matey! Scare me away? No way will that happen. You don't seem to have a clue as to how much you've always meant to me. And know this—I don't scare very easily. That is not to say I don't have a lot on my plate right now because I do."

Matt goes on, explaining that he's extremely busy running for office, that his schedule changes constantly, and that he's also helping a friend finish a home repair project. "Please understand I have a virtual smorgasbord on my plate right now, and I hope you'll bear with me during this busy time."

Of course I will bear with him! And I'm so relieved to hear his voice that I babble. "It's no wonder you have no time to call or write with all you have going on. You're juggling a lot and still willing to take on more. It's not surprising that you have so many friends, Matt, and I am flattered you feel I contributed to that."

"Contributed? Heck, until we started working together and I began walking you home from work, I was a loner. I'd never before been part of a neighborhood or a group of people until you introduced me to your friends. You were the catalyst for the entire direction my life was to take."

I suddenly forget that gravity has begun to do some nasty work to my boobs and butt, and some grey has snuck in to streak my auburn hair. And so what if I'm not working downtown? We can meet anywhere. I clear my throat. "I'd like us to get together, Matt, and I'm looking forward to seeing you after all these years."

"I have a busy week coming up, but I'll be in the city on Tuesday for a breakfast meeting. Assuming my schedule doesn't change, would a last-minute call to get together for lunch on Tuesday work for you?"

He's lifted my heart since we reconnected. "I'll make it work, Matt. When I told you that you were spoiling me with your emails, I meant it."

"Truth be told, all I'm doing is telling you I am very grateful to you. You opened so many doors for me because of the simple thing you did for me when we were young people, and that was being my friend."

I want to run my fingers through his red hair and kiss him hard on his lips.

"I'll pick you up for lunch on Tuesday," he says, "so text me your address."

I do, and we say our good nights. I hang up the phone and get ready for bed, all the while thinking about Matt and wondering where we might be headed.

Before I hit the sack, I send Matt an email:

I wake up mornings anxious to open my email to see if you've written. I feel like a smitten teenager and plan to see you in my dreams.

I click Send, and immediately wish I could pull the email back. We haven't even gotten together, and I've nearly told him I'm in love. Maybe I am or will be, but I can't possibly know that yet. But the email's been sent, so there's no use dwelling on it. I turn off my computer and fall asleep thinking of Matt.

~ * ~

I'm naked and asleep when dream Matt comes to tuck me in, and I feel him crawl into my bed and lie beside me. He's also naked, and tonight he holds me in his arms, my back to his front. My wet begins to flow when I feel his dick pressing against my ass.

His dick is as large and hard as it always is in my dreams, and tonight is no exception. He penetrates me from behind, and I gyrate my hips to match his pace. I shudder when waves of orgasm overwhelm me, and I feel dream Matt climax as well.

He turns me toward him and sucks my nipples, and a wave of wet courses through me. "I'm glad you came to bed naked," he tells me.

He's hard again and plunges into me. We make love once more, and then dream Matt is gone.

Chapter Three

I remember my dream when I awaken the next morning. I'm having better sex in my dreams than I had in real life and wonder how that's possible.

I can hardly wait to check my phone to see if Matt sent me an email. He did, and there it is in black and white:

Whoa Nellie, "smitten?" Planning to see me in your dreams?

I feel my heart sink. I was feeling giddy and bursting with happiness when I wrote that email, so I wrote exactly what I felt in my heart at that moment. But after I sent the email, I worried that I said too much, too soon. As I suspected I might have done, I'd gone too far. And then the phone rings.

It's Matt. "So, what did we do in your dreams, Kaity?"

There's no way in hell I can tell him what we did in my dreams, and I'm lost in my reverie of hot steamy sex.

"Kaity? Smitten?"

"As soon as I sent that email last night, I wished I could have pulled it back."

"Why would you want to pull it back?"

"I thought I might have been too forward. What I was trying to say, Matt, is you have put a smile on my face, brought happiness back into my life."

"Don't you think you do that for me as well? Because do you ever. You don't realize how much I care about you. You made my heart flutter to think you had good thoughts of me."

Now it's my turn to feel my heart flutter. "I find myself daydreaming again, and it's been a long time since I allowed myself to dream."

"I hope I can help make your dreams come true," he says, "and that your daydreams are plentiful and awesome. I hope you'll tell me all about them and your overnight dreams as well."

Right. As if I can tell him that we loved the last several nights away. I wish I could, but I don't know how. "I will do my best to share my dreams with you."

"I want you to know, Kaity, that you can share with me *anything*, even your most intimate thoughts. You can be completely honest with me."

"Honesty is very important to me, and I want and hope that whatever happens between us will be honest and loving, whether it's intimacy or companionship we share."

"If I may be so bold, I have so many intimate thoughts I would like to share with you because you conjure up so much within me. I'm not talking about sex, although I'd be a liar not to say I think you are absolutely gorgeous and have an absolutely desirable to-die-for body."

Uh-oh, he *is* still thinking of me as my former sixteen-year-old self. I need to set him straight. "Matt, I am no longer the teenage beauty you are remembering."

"Kaity, you will always look the same to me, and I would melt if ever you were to offer yourself to me."

Did I hear him right? My heart is stuck in my throat, and I'm unable to speak.

"But I realize you wanting to be intimate with me isn't going to happen. It's a fact I've resolved myself to."

No! That's crazy! I don't want him to even *think* about making such a ludicrous resolution. "Why would you think that, Matt? That's ridiculous."

"It is?" Matt sort of laughs and says, "No kidding?"

I swallow hard and the words come to me. "I dream of you tucking me in at night, and whatever else happens, happens."

"Whoa Nellie! We agree we can say and ask each other anything, right?"

"That's right."

"In that case, will you be naked?"

Holey Moley. "Completely." Just as I've been in my dreams.

Chapter Four

It's Thursday, and my face hurts from smiling all the time. I can hardly wait until Tuesday when Matt and I will finally get together.

I send him an email:

I love writing to you, Matt, and reading your emails make my day.

Matt responds:

I can't wait until I can hold you in my arms on Tuesday, Kaity. You can't imagine how much I want to hold you.

And I reply:

And I want so much to be in your arms.

I'm almost certain there's something going on between us. My heart feels lighter, and I think I might be falling in love. This kitten is smitten.

Matt asks in his next email:

Would you like to be graphic? If so, please have at it. Be as graphic as you like. Tell me how you want me to make love to you.

Holy Smokes! I think about his large hands and long fingers and wish I knew how to tell him what I'm thinking at this moment. Instead, I respond with:

I've been dreaming of making love to you for days, Matt. I want to tell you how I want you to make love to me, but I don't know how to do that.

He writes in response:

Then I'll tell you what will happen after our lunch on Tuesday. We'll go somewhere private, and I'll take you into my arms and hold you. I'm going to kiss and caress you, and I'll kiss you again and again. I'll unbutton your blouse, and my lips will work their way from your neck to your shoulder and down to your beautiful breasts. I'll get on my knees and lift your skirt, Kaity, and I will kiss my way up your thighs. Finally, I will get there, and I will tantalize you. In the next moment, I'll enter you slowly, and I expect it won't take long before we climax together.

Matt's email ends with a question:

Will you be ready to make love with me FOR REAL on Tuesday?

I can't remember ever being so ready for anything in my life. And that's what I tell him.

Chapter Five

Today is Friday, and I haven't heard from Matt yet today. I know he's busy, but I miss him. What has happened to the logical, rational person who is supposed to be doing legal research? Rather than doing the work I'm supposed to be doing, I went for a run in the heat and humidity of a summer afternoon in Chicago and ran until I was gasping for breath. And now I'm sitting in my kitchen chugging water and daydreaming about a guy I haven't seen in decades, wishing I could feel his arms around me.

Realizing I need to get my ass in gear, I shower and change clothes. I get back to work, and I'm sitting at my computer, storming Lexis and Westlaw, doing the research I'm supposed to be doing and lost in my work, when Matt emails:

> *I have to work a booth for a national political party at the Pocah County Fair and won't have time to write or talk today.*

It's just as well. I want to complete my assignment so that I'll be free to get together with Matt on Tuesday.

Four more days.

Chapter Six

Saturday arrives. In an early morning call, Matt mentions he has a list of errands to run and chores to do today. He also tells me he'll probably be working the booth again at the Pocah County Fair, which means he won't have time to talk or write, but surprise, surprise, he just texted me:

Good morning. I've been thinking about you all night, Kaity, and I decided to put my thoughts in a letter to you.

A letter? Hmmm. Why not just tell me what he's thinking? Regardless of how he chooses to tell me his thoughts, I hope they are good ones. Without mentioning his thoughts or his letter, I reply:

Good morning to you, too. I got up early, and I've been working on my research assignment for most of the morning.

His next text reads:

I'm going to get my chores and errands done, and then I'm going to end the day by finishing my letter to you. So, until later, Sending love.

This time I respond mentioning both his letter and his thoughts:

I'm looking forward to receiving your letter. Will you give me a hint of why you want to put your thoughts in writing? Also sending love.

Matt calls a few minutes later. "The purpose of writing this letter is to let you know how important it is to me that you helped me lay the foundation for the rest of my life."

My heart swells. "I can't wait to read it, Matt."

"I've got to run so I can get my work done, but let's talk later."

I spend the rest of the afternoon doing research, and my assignment is coming along nicely. At the rate I'm going, I expect I'll finish later today and then have the next couple of days free to daydream about Matt and decide on what to wear when we get together on Tuesday.

I complete my assignment by the time night falls and place my research into file folders. I turn off my computer and printer and stand and stretch. I go to the kitchen to get a bottle of water from the fridge, uncap it and take a long drink.

Matt telephones a short time later. "Hi Kaity, I've run my errands and finished my chores. As expected, I have to go work the booth at the County Fair for a while. It's just one of the many things that go hand in hand with running for office in the township. Before I head over there, I was hoping you would help me with something."

"Sure, if I can, I'll be glad to," I say.

"When I said you could share with me anything, even your most intimate thoughts, you said I could do the same. And you told me that honesty was very important to you, and you wanted and hoped whatever happened between us would be honest and loving, whether it was intimacy or companionship we would share. Do you remember saying that?"

I wonder why he's asking, but of course I remember. "Yes, I remember."

"Could you elaborate on what you were trying to convey with the words, 'whether it's intimacy or companionship we share?'"

I don't know where he's going with this, but an uneasy feeling is slithering its way into my heart.

Matt continues. "I have a reasonable idea of what this means, of course, but I'd appreciate if you would tell me what message you were trying to convey. Perhaps you were saying, 'I'll take whatever piece or pieces of you that you are willing to share with me,' or something like, 'however we can fit into each other's lives would be—what?' You fill in the blank. There are so many directions those words can take, Kaity, so what say you?"

I say nothing, that's what I say. Have I misread the signals or read more than was warranted into our recent calls and emails because I'm starved for affection? Maybe there's nothing happening between us after all. And it isn't only my heart that's feeling uneasy. My stomach muscles are tense because it sounds like maybe Matt is having second thoughts about our reconnection, and I'm at a loss for words.

"This will help me with the letter I am writing," Matt says, "because it will serve to tell me where you are in life and happiness and how best to move forward with my letter."

Feeling my stomach muscles clinch and clench, I take a deep breath and try to explain. "I meant that I hoped we could and would be part of one another's lives in any way possible."

I sigh and go on. "Maybe I can better answer your question if I tell you that I felt a spark during our first telephone call, and that spark has grown stronger and brighter with each and every call, text or email we've shared. You've awakened something in me that I thought was gone forever, Matt, and it feels good to feel alive again. I'm extremely passionate and loving, caring and giving, and I believe that intimacy is the ideal and best way to express and share those kinds of feelings."

I sip from my water bottle. "I have a lot more I want to share with you, whether we remain friends or become lovers." I'm on the verge of tears, but I'm a big girl and won't cry. I take several long gulps of water and clear my throat before saying, "But I will settle for friendship if that's what you have to offer." I finish the water and ask, "Does that answer your question?"

"I have so much to share with you. Good night for now," Matt says and ends the call.

I undress and take a quick shower before climbing into bed. As far as I'm concerned, it is *not* better to have loved and lost than never to have loved at all. Never having loved would be so much easier.

I fall asleep while tears dampen my pillow.

Chapter Seven

Matt calls late Saturday night, and I pick up the phone in my bedroom. "I hope I didn't wake you, Kaity, but I just got home. I've been thinking about you all evening, and I have a question."

My pillow is still wet with my tears, and I sit up in bed. I hope it isn't another question about companionship. I clear my throat to get the sleep out of my voice. "What's the question, Matt?"

"Do you like having your nipples kissed?"

Maybe I'm still asleep and dreaming. I pinch myself. Ow! Nope, I'm not dreaming. "Yes!"

"Tell me about your fantasies," he says.

I haven't had any fantasies in a long time. I've sort of given up on that particular aspect of my life. "I need to think about that for a bit."

"I want you to tell me," Matt insists.

Fully awake now, I say, "This is new to me, Matt. Would dreaming about making love to you be a fantasy?"

"Definitely. How long has it been since you've been intimate with someone?"

Intimate? It's been a long, lonely time for true intimacy. I can't even guess how long it's been. "Intimacy is a distant memory, Matt."

"I'm guessing you had sex during your marriage."

I suppose that's technically true. But it's not even close to true in terms of what I consider to be enjoyable sex, and I sigh before I answer. "It's been about six years since I last had enjoyable sex."

"Whoa Nellie! *Six years*?"

"Six years. I told myself I didn't care about sex anymore, and then you came along and breathed life into me."

"Six years is a long time, Kaity," he says.

Ya' think?

"Fucking you will be like fucking a virgin," Matt says.

I gasp and feel wet gather between my thighs.

"How wild do you like to get?" he asks.

"Tell me what something wild would be so I can answer you honestly."

"For instance, would it turn you on if I pulled the car over to the side of the road and we fucked in the car?"

I'm going to need another shower after listening to Matt. A cold one this time.

"What about naughty talk? Do you like to talk naughty?"

Hmmm. I've heard about it and have been somewhat titillated by it in some of the books I enjoy, but naughty talk has not been a part of my own sexual experience. "I don't know how to talk naughty, Matt."

"It will be my pleasure to teach you," he says. "I want to fuck you."

Whoa and Holey Moley. I feel my face redden.

"Come on, Kaity, talk naughty. Repeat after me. I want to fuck you."

Those five words are words I've used before, of course, but never together in the same sentence. What the hell is my problem? I'm an adult. "I want to fuck you," I repeat. Despite being an adult, my ears can hardly believe the words that just came out of my mouth, and my skin becomes gooseflesh.

"There you go," he says. "Being naughty isn't so difficult, is it?"

Surprised I got the words out at all, I answer, "Not as difficult as I thought it would be."

"Kaity, do you know what a queen is?"

"Assuming you don't mean Elizabeth, what is a queen?"

"There's an old adage that puts forth the theory that whores like to be treated like queens in the bedroom, and queens like to be treated like whores in the bedroom. You're obviously not a whore, so you must be a queen. Have you ever thought about being treated like a naughty girl in the bedroom?"

No way, no how. "I'm willing to do most anything, and I am very sexual and enjoy mutually satisfying sex. But gentle foreplay and being treated with love and respect is important to me. Getting slapped around doesn't appeal to me. Not at all. I am not a queen, Matt, and I don't think we're on the same page about this stuff."

"I would never be abusive, Kaity. I asked because I believe knowing what a lover likes and doesn't like is a good rule of thumb for being a good lover. I would always treat you with love and respect. We are definitely on the same page."

That's comforting. Feeling reassured, I yawn.

"It's late, Kaity. You should get some sleep."

A quick glance at the clock tells me it's nearly midnight. "When are you going to send me the letter you're writing?"

"When I finish writing it, I'll send it."

Feeling foolish for asking a question with such an obvious answer, I change the subject and say, "Wishing you sweet dreams, Matt."

"Sleep well, my precious," he replies.

I hang up the phone and go back to sleep with Matt on my mind.

Chapter Eight

Rain falls hard, and the hours between midnight and morning are filled with lightning slashing the skies and the clashing of thunder. I fantasize about making love with Matt throughout the stormy night and dream of being held in his arms.

After I shower and dress Sunday morning, I write to Matt:

We had quite the storm last night, and the thunder was almost as loud as the pounding of my heart—as well as some other pounding I fantasized about. I thought about you most of the night, wishing I was in your arms, wanting you to hold me.

I don't think I realized how lonely I was, Matt, and then a miracle happened when you contacted me. It's as if you brought a breath of fresh air back into my life, and I feel alive again. I hope we'll take the chance to build a relationship, to share our lives, and perhaps grow old together. Sending love, Kaity.

Matt responds:

As far as the pounding you want me to give you, just how much sex can you handle in a day? How do you like to be fucked? When I have sex, it's very important to me to make my partner come even before I do, and that's why I'm asking these kinds of questions. I hope I haven't offended you with my naughty talk.

Holy Smokes!

Not long after sending his email, Matt calls. "Am I being offensive or does this naughty talk turn you on?"

"It's a whole 'nother world you've opened to me."

"How bad do you want me to fuck you, Kaity?"

BAD in capital letters, but I play it down a bit. "Bad with a capital B."

"Do you like being on top when you fuck?" he asks.

On top, on the bottom, sideways, standing up, sitting down. "Any position is okay with me."

"Do you like having your nipples sucked when you fuck?"

"Even when I'm not being fucked," I answer.

"I've got to run now," Matt says, "but let's talk later."

~ * ~

I email Matt:

I can't wait to make love to you, and I'm going to remember every moment when I fantasize you are tucking me in at night.

Matt responds:

Hey, Kaity. I want to take a moment to tell you how exciting it is when you talk to me about tucking you into bed. I suspect you're saying you wish I was there to fuck you in every way possible. Tell me more about your fantasies.

Holey Moley. I should have waited to take my shower and made it a cold one. I respond:

Making love to you is mostly what I fantasize about. And you are spot on about what I want when I wish you were tucking me in. I cannot wait until I am in your arms, and we make our fantasies come to life.

Matt writes:

I was lying in bed thinking about you, Kaity, all the way back to September 7th, all those years ago when we first met. Two innocent kids who became friends. Maybe because I didn't feel worthy of you, I didn't fantasize about us being together. Even when I first contacted you, I didn't have those thoughts. How things have changed and so rapidly. Isn't it crazy we are suddenly having these intense feelings for one another and conversing as sensually as we are? How the heck did that happen?

And then he calls. "Have you ever before been so quick to want to give yourself to someone?"

"It's never happened before."

"Add to that the sensuality, the naughty talk," Matt says. "I've always wanted to have a partner to whom I could talk naughty and who would get excited by it the way I do. When did you first start thinking about me fucking you?"

I thought about it when we were teenagers, but I'm not going to admit it. Instead, I tell him, "I'm not sure."

After our phone call, I sit down and write to Matt:

As I told you, it's been about six years since I enjoyed true intimacy. At some point, I wrapped up all my intimate thoughts, dreams and fantasies and tucked them safely away. I hardly ever thought about sex unless I was reading a novel with a love scene or watching one in a movie or on TV.

But then you came along and put a spell on me, or bewitched me or something, and all those thoughts, dreams and fantasies have burst out and are now on a rampage. Tell me what you want me to do to you. What do YOU fantasize about?

Matt responds:

I know you're an absolutely respectable and honorable person, but I love how you've opened yourself up to me. You're on track with my fantasies, and our naughty talk really turns me on.

On the serious side, though, please know that, while I want to do all these things to you, it's just bedroom talk, and I would NEVER EVER disrespect you outside of the bedroom.

As far as I'm concerned, Tuesday cannot come quickly enough.

Chapter Nine

I wake up early on a sunny Monday morning in July with Matt on my mind. I already exercised and showered—mostly a cold one—and I'm going through my closet, pulling out clothes and trying them on, trying to decide which outfit is the most flattering when the phone rings. It's Matt.

"Good morning, beautiful. I'm lying here in bed this morning thinking of when I called you when you first moved back to Chicago. Heck, I was living just a mile away from you then. I was married at the time, but as passionate as we are about each other today, I wonder if we'd have been lovers if we'd gotten together during those years."

What might have been. "I don't doubt it would have been wonderful, Matt, but I wouldn't have interfered in your marriage."

"Could I have talked you into letting us get passionate with each other if I told you how unhappy I was?"

Probably not, but I don't really know. "I was vulnerable at the time, so maybe you could have persuaded me. But I do wish we'd gotten together at some point when we were younger."

"Truth be told," Matt says, "younger, yes. However, not as young as sixteen because neither one of us would have had the life experiences we have had. It likely would have spelled disaster for us just like it did for others who thought their puppy loves would last forever. Yourself included."

Ouch! But I have to admit that he's right to realize that marrying too young is often a disaster waiting to happen, and that I am a prime example of why it isn't a good idea. "I was thinking more along the lines of before I lost my mind and moved to San Francisco, Matt. That's the 'younger' I was wishing about."

"I cannot begin to tell you how much I would have liked that, Kaity. I was unhappy for so long that I forgot what it was like to be happy."

So, marriage was no picnic for him either. "Marriage can be scary when it doesn't work."

"That's for sure. I believe the final straw was when my ex got angry that I wanted to get involved with some community activities and compete in the police and fire department Olympics. She despised the idea of me getting involved with the community so much that she insisted we go to marriage counseling."

Matt sighs. "We went to six different marriage counselors, all of them female. Every counselor advised her to support me, but nothing and nobody could change her mind. Her disappointment with the results of the counseling probably was what led her to file for divorce."

He pauses for a beat and then continues talking. "My divorce was almost as scary as the marriage. We were able to work things out, but the divorce was costly—but worth the cost because I was so miserable."

He sighs again, longer and deeper this time. "So yes, I wish we would have gotten together sooner. I think we could have had a wonderful life together, and hooking up with you earlier would have been so comforting."

"For me too, Matt, because if we'd gotten back in touch *before* I met my second husband, you might have saved me from myself."

"Since we're back in touch now, Kaity, let's not waste any more time."

"Let's not," I agree.

"What I truly want to do is hold you and kiss you and let ourselves get passionate with one another. I also want us to have a serious conversation. I just don't know which direction to go first. What thoughts do you have?"

As of late, my thoughts are mostly naughty ones, but I answer, "I'm not sure."

"Here's the most important thing for me. I don't want to lose track of what my whole focus was when I first contacted you. That is the paramount factor here. And I want to make love to you, Kaity, but I think we need to first spend some time having a serious conversation."

Matt probably is right, and I agree it would be a good idea for us to first have a serious conversation. As long as serious lovemaking follows our serious conversation, I'm all for it. Seriously.

Chapter Ten

I got Matt's letter today:

Dear Kaity,

Here's the letter I've been working on. There is so much to say and so much to catch up on. However, what I want to do first is thank you for what you contributed to my life, which was my original focus in contacting you.

As you know, I was sixteen years old when I got my job at the grocery store. The date was September 7th, the day I met you, and the purpose of this writing is to explain how you helped lay the foundation for the rest of my life.

You opened up a whole new world to me with your friendship, and I finally had the confidence I needed to make friends of my own. I developed a strong work ethic, learned to look people in the eye, and to be honest, thoughtful, and considerate. I made it my goal to go above and beyond with a good attitude and respect for others. There are five men in my life who influenced the direction my life was to take. You are the only woman to have influenced me so greatly, and I thank you for that.

I'm so touched that I have to pause reading for a moment. And then my eyes go back to Matt's letter:

I honestly did not—not even for a fleeting moment— ever think of anything other than to contact you to say thank you. I was hoping this would make you feel good about yourself, and it might be something you could take with you to give you continued hope that there is goodness in this world. It would also bring closure to me that I reached out to you to say thank you because it was that important to me. I am blessed that I believe you are the last person to be thanked.

It's really simple—I don't want to leave this earth with regrets I didn't contact everyone who made me who I am. I am no longer afraid to express my appreciation because someone might consider it corny. I feel it is of paramount importance that people, such as yourself, are thanked.

Throughout my life, I've had friends who have come through for me when I was in need. I've done my best to let them know I appreciate their showing of love. I can never pay them back, but I pay it forward to others, and those who have helped me know that's what I do. Since this has been the story of my life, it's ingrained in me to always thank those who have helped me.

And here we are, Kaity, innocently approaching another turn in our lives. I love that we care deeply for one another and desire each other, and I hope to meet every desire you may have.

Maybe not so fast, though, for I have to tell you something that could change the direction we've been moving in as abruptly as it started. Until as recently as last month, I was involved with a woman I've known for a long time. It was just by chance we got together. We ran into each other while I was visiting out-of-town friends after my divorce. One thing led to another, and she moved in with me.

But then last month, the relationship collapsed. She's going to have to find somewhere else to live but continues to reside with me while she collects her thoughts and decides where she wants to go.

There are many reasons that having a relationship with her won't work. We were just supposed to be Traveling Partners, and it turned into a "sort of" relationship. Marriage was never talked about. Instead, we referred to ourselves as Traveling Partners because that was the mutual goal we shared. We were intimate until the relationship ended but haven't been since.

You told me that I brought a breath of fresh air into your life. Well, ditto for me, but there never seemed to be an opportunity to talk about current relationships because things between us rapidly spiraled in the direction they did because of the tremendous emotions we share.

I feel terrible now because our little tryst the past few days may have gotten out of hand. Oh sure, I LOVED the naughty talk and all. Perhaps my need for someone played a huge part as well, just as it might have done for you. If you recall, you told me that maybe you could have been persuaded to get together with me when you returned to Chicago because of your vulnerability. Well, my vulnerability weakened me, and I apologize for that.

I have no idea what direction my life will take now. Do you still want to get together tomorrow to see if we can build a relationship? Or, if as you wrote, would you be willing to take any option you are availed, intimacy or companionship? What are your thoughts? Your response would be appreciated.

Sending love,

Matt

Chapter Eleven

I respond to Matt's letter with a letter of my own:

Dear Matt,

I am flattered to think our friendship made a difference in your life, and I'm happy to have been the good influence you believe me to have been.

You told me you're not certain what direction you want your life to take at this time. I will be good with friendship, companionship, whatever you have to offer. But that doesn't change that I long to be in your arms, and it's important to me that you know that. I need to share with you the thoughts of my heart.

You've opened up a whole new hopeful world for me, and I hope that I'll be able to do that for you as well. I want to learn so much more about you and your life, and I have so much more to tell you about mine. We became friends the moment we met, and it feels, at least to me, as though all our "missed" years have fallen away, disappeared, vanished, and that you walked me home from work just yesterday.

As for the rest, thank you for being honest. It's so important because honesty is the basis of trust and the foundation on which a relationship is built. A relationship cannot succeed without it. As I believe you know, I speak from personal experience.

Things between us did happen rather quickly, and I suppose it's understandable you didn't say anything until now. I wish, though, that your "sort of" relationship would have been brought into the open before our "tryst" got out of hand, which would have been so much better than finding out about it now.

You said there are many reasons why your relationship with your Traveling Partner won't work. Will you tell me what happened to make you want to end the relationship? How long do you expect her to continue living with you? Perhaps most importantly, what are your feelings for her?

I obviously need to know the answers to these questions because if we are going to try to build our own relationship, I will put everything I have into it. I will give you all of me in every way. You have made me come alive again, and I'm happier than I've been in a very long time.

I want you in my life, Matt. I need you in my life. I don't want to stop thinking about you. I don't want to stop looking for your emails. I don't want to stop waiting for you to call. I don't want to go to sleep without dreaming about you. I don't even think I can stop.

If companionship is all you can offer, I'll accept that. But if we might have a chance to build a relationship and someday grow old together, then, hell yes, let's see what happens when we get together tomorrow.
Sending love,
Kaity

Chapter Twelve

Matt emails a response to my letter:

To tell you the truth, Kaity, I am absolutely—I want to say dumbfounded, but I think I will use another word— bewildered by your response that you are STILL WILLING to have me—what sounds like COMPLETELY—in your life when I would have been happy just being a small part of your life as a friend.

In one sense, I feel ashamed I didn't tell you about my "sort of" relationship. I wondered if I was deceiving you by not bringing it up, but I felt there was no need since that was not my purpose in contacting you. When things started getting hot and heavy, I began to wonder, am I deceiving Kaity? Lying to her? I told myself "no" since, as I said, going in that direction was never my intention. Besides, the relationship I was in was over.

Know, though, I certainly never thought YOU would want ME in your life, so I felt confident that the topic could be put on the back burner until we got together to talk in person. I knew I was at least approaching the line when I started changing the dialogue to our soft porn conversation.

As far as your questions, if I may, I'd like to save that conversation for tomorrow so that I can answer any and all of your questions face to face. I hope we're still on for lunch, and I'll call you after my breakfast meeting. Are we still getting a room tomorrow? Sending love, Matt.

And I respond:

Please take me down from the pedestal you have me on. I don't deserve to be up there. I think having me up there on that pedestal is the reason you're feeling dumbfounded or bewildered that I would be willing to have you in my life. I liked you when we met. If I knew then what I know now, I'd have done my darndest to make you mine all those long years ago. Because I would love to have you in my life— completely.

I'm always willing to give more than I get—which has often gotten me into trouble—and I've made terrible, awful mistakes. I think I was ready to give up on happiness for a while there. But then came you. When I tell you that you brought me back to life, I mean that since our first phone call, I feel alive again. YOU make me feel alive. I want YOU to want ME.

If you told me you were involved with somebody when we first talked, I wouldn't have let myself think we could be more than friends. I don't know exactly when I felt my heart opening to you, but I wouldn't have allowed myself to hope for a relationship with you if I knew you were involved with somebody else.

But it would be a shame, I think, not to get together after reconnecting after so many years, so let's keep our lunch date tomorrow. If nothing else, it will be good to see you again. Sending love, Kaity.

~ * ~

Matt emails me again later:

The least we can do is talk.

Attached to his email is a copy of the hotel reservation he made.

I am acutely aware that I don't always make good decisions or make the right choices in my personal life. I *might* regret if things between us don't work out, but I'm absolutely *certain* I would regret not taking the chance. Because I believe—or want to believe—that whatever is happening between us is both real and right.

I can't help but wonder if I've lost my mind again. I hope not, but I fall asleep dreaming of Matt.

Chapter Thirteen

It's finally Tuesday, and I can't wait to see Matt. I have a hard time deciding what to wear and keep changing my mind and my clothing, so it takes me hours to get dressed. I think about putting my hair into a ponytail, but I mousse it instead and scrunch it into loose curls for a sexier look. I insert small gold hoops into my earlobes. My easiest decision is choosing not to wear a bra. Because the outdoor temperature is ninety-plus degrees, I settle on wearing navy blue silky shorts and a sleeveless blue print blouse.

Matt calls to say he's on his way to pick me up for lunch and expects to arrive within a half hour. I'm so excited that, even though it's so hot out, I sit outside on the front porch anxiously awaiting his arrival.

He pulls into my driveway and gets out of his car. He's as handsome as I remember, maybe even more so, with a touch of grey in his red hair, although perhaps a shade lighter than the fiery red it was once upon a time. He's wearing tan Dockers and a green short-sleeved shirt. My heart is beating so rapidly it feels like it might burst from my chest.

We walk toward one another and embrace, and he smiles with eyes the gentle blue that I remember. Matt is about a head taller than I am, and he leans down to kiss me. It's a long, languid, delicious kiss, and already I can feel the wet beginning to flow between my legs.

Still embracing, he smiles and says, "Hey, Kaity, that was our first real kiss."

And what a kiss it was! "It's so good to see you after all this time, Matt."

"You look wonderful, just the way you looked when you were sixteen years old. Still gorgeous and still desirable."

I blush, and he kisses me again and says, "Let's grab lunch," and he walks me to his car. When I'm seat-belted, he closes the door and goes around and gets into the driver's seat. "Where to?"

I hadn't even thought about where to go for lunch but then remember a nearby coffee shop. "Uh, there's a coffee shop about a half mile away."

"That sounds good to me."

I give him directions, and Matt leans toward me, and we kiss again. I hope with all my heart I'm wide awake and not dreaming.

The coffee shop is only minutes away, and Matt comes around to the passenger side of my car to open the door for me when we arrive. We hold hands as we walk to the restaurant entrance. We're seated and given menus when I realize I'm not the least bit hungry. And didn't Matt just come from a breakfast meeting?

"What are you going to have?" he asks me.

"Coffee," I say. "I'm not hungry. Are you?"

"Not really. I'll have lemonade."

The waitress stops by and takes our beverage orders. She goes to get our drinks, and Matt says, "I believe I owe you the answers to some questions you have, and I'd like to get that part of our conversation out of the way."

I'm on pins and needles waiting for him to answer my questions about the end of his Traveling Partner relationship.

"I travel in my RV, and there's often work to be done when traveling," he explains. "During the last several trips we took, my Traveling Partner went off the deep end when I needed help with something. She told me she'd 'had it,' that she 'didn't want to do this anymore,' that she 'was done,' screeching out the words. I decided I no longer wanted to deal with her histrionics."

Our beverages arrive, and Matt pauses in his narrative to add sugar to his lemonade. He continues. "Another thing is that she's not at all supportive. Not of me or of my ambitions. She refused to even accompany me to the courthouse when I was put on the ballot. Can you believe that? I realized I didn't want her in my life anymore, and that a serious relationship with her would never work. I talked to her about it, and she agreed that we should end it. Now it's just a matter of her deciding where she wants to go."

Matt looks me in the eye and says, "I'm relieved that our Traveling Partnership has come to an end."

Be still my heart. I want to run around the table, sit on his lap and kiss him long and hard. Of course I don't do that, and we spend the next half hour chatting about the hot weather and other inconsequential things, neither of us saying a word about where we are heading next. I'm so nervous that I have to hold my coffee cup with both hands to prevent the coffee from spilling over the rim of the cup.

The waitress comes over to top off my coffee and tells us the coffee shop is getting ready to close for the day.

"It's only three o'clock and they're closing?" Matt asks.

I can't believe I picked probably the only place in town that closes in midafternoon. "Sorry about that," I say.

"No need to apologize," Matt says, "but let's get the heck out of here. Are you ready?"

As I would ever be.

~ * ~

Matt and I arrive at the hotel and check in, holding hands as we walk up the corridor to the elevator. We enter the waiting car, and Matt smiles at me. I can't wait to be in his arms, and I'm filled with anticipation and flowing with wet with the realization that we are about to make love.

"Are you nervous?" he asks me.

"Close to having a breakdown," I tell him.

We both laugh, sort of nervously.

The elevator door closes, and Matt bends to kiss me as the elevator makes its ascent. When we arrive at our floor, we walk down the corridor to our room. Matt unlocks the door, and we go inside.

We hold hands and look at one another. "We need to have our serious conversation, Kaity," Matt says and walks me over to the bed. We sit and he continues talking. "I want you to know what a paramount role you've played in my life, and how grateful I am to you. Do you realize how important it is to me that you know that? *Really know that.* And do you also realize how special you are to me and how much I care about you?"

I find it difficult to speak, but I have words that need to be said, and that Matt needs to hear. "I do, Matt, and I understand it's important to you to *know* that I do. And I hope you *also* realize how special you are to me, and how much I care about you."

He takes me into his arms and kisses me. We undress and climb into bed together. We get under the blankets, and we're lying side by side. It's finally going to happen, and every nerve in my body is tingling.

Matt takes my hand and moves it beneath the blankets and places it on his groin. "Feel how hard I am, Kaity."

His dick is large and hard, and his hand covers mine. I begin to massage him, his hand moving with my own, and the wet pours out of me. His lips go to my neck and move toward my shoulder, sending shivers throughout my body, and then his tongue finds the nipple of my breast, first one and then the other. His tongue darts and dances, and a wave of pleasure rocks my body as I feel him becoming fully erect beneath my fingers.

Matt throws off the blankets and moves above me. I open wide my legs and watch him put his big dick into me, and my wet flows. He thrusts, and I cry out. He thrusts again and his cock goes deeper, and then he begins to pound. I move with him, matching him thrust for thrust, as he pushes deeper into me and pumps and pounds harder. And then an amazing orgasm makes its way through my entire body at the same time Matt shudders and climaxes. It's even better than the way I dreamed it would be, and we hold each other at its culmination.

Feeling warm and fuzzy in the aftermath of our lovemaking, I say, "Matt, this place could be our Love Nest."

He laughs and says, "Seriously?"

"Don't make fun."

He hugs me and says, "Sorry. Let's give it a code name. We'll call it LN1," and we laugh together.

It's late, and I know that Matt is exhausted. I massage his feet until he falls asleep. When he's sleeping soundly, I lie down beside him and whisper in his ear words I'm not courageous enough to say aloud in the light of day because they are words I don't think he's ready to hear. But here in the dark, while he's sleeping peacefully and can't hear me, it feels safe to tell him. "You are the man of my dreams, Matt. You are honest and ethical, hardworking and trustworthy. You have the courage to stand up for your beliefs, and you are a loyal and true friend to many. I've fallen in love with you. I don't know how it happened, but, some day, I hope we will share our lives and grow old together."

I want to believe that maybe the third time will be the charm for me, and that, someday there might be a happily ever after in my future.

Chapter Fourteen

Matt and I both have busy schedules during the next few weeks, but spend most of our free time together, sometimes going to lunch or dinner, and almost always making love. I keep wanting him to spend the night, but he always goes home to prepare for whatever's on his schedule the next day.

July ends, and it's suddenly a new month. And August is an even busier month than was July.

Matt has a lot of work to do to free himself up before he goes on a two-week fishing trip with his buddies. They're heading way up north to a little island in Canada's Lake of the Woods, and they'll have to survive two weeks without internet, cellphones or television.

The trial for which I did research and prepared case summaries is set to get underway, and I'm a member of the trial team that travels to Boston. I love working with this team, headed by Zach Eberle, the partner in charge. Zach is beloved by the entire team for his consideration and good humor, and because he works himself every bit as hard as he works each of us.

It's one of the last days of August when I return to Chicago after the parties settle just before verdict. The good news is that the settlement is in favor of WAM's client.

In other good news, Matt calls to say he's back from Canada and has cellphone and internet service again.

"Hey, Kaity, I missed you and want to see you. It's a beautiful summer night. We probably won't have many more of these before the cooler weather sets in. Would you be up for a walk along a deserted beach tonight?"

I missed him, too, and it will be good to finally get together again. "Oooh. A deserted beach sounds like a fine idea," I happily reply.

"Do you want to have dinner first?"

"How about fast food later? I just got a new work assignment, and I'd like to get started on it."

"That'll work. I'll pick you up at eight-thirty."

"Perfect. I can't wait to see you."

"Ditto," he says. "See you soon."

~ * ~

Although darkness has fallen, the evening is still warm as Matt and I walk hand in hand along a deserted beach. We stop to spread our blanket onto the sand and sit down and remove our clothing. We tumble onto the blanket, and lay head to feet and feet to head, our lips, our tongues, our mouths working together, our touches and tastes continuing to parallel one another, me to him and him to me. Except for moonlight and starshine, it's a dance in the darkness.

Waves of wet race through my body, as each of us give and share our energy with the other. Then Matt changes position and moves above me. He enters me just as a water wave washes over us, but our own waves are a tsunami, our rhythm phenomenal. So in tune are we, so marvelous together, we create our own symphony. We climax together moments later and lie in each other's arms, gazing up at the stars and basking in the light of the moon.

~ * ~

Matt brings me home and walks me to my door. We embrace and kiss good night. "We didn't pick up fast food. Would you like to come in and have something to eat?"

"I've got a long drive ahead of me and should get going."

"You're welcome to stay the night," I offer.

"I wish I could, but I've got an early meeting tomorrow that I have to prepare for tonight."

"I loved our walk along the beach, Matt."

"Same here, Kaity."

"Tomorrow?" I ask.

"For sure," he answers and kisses me again before he leaves to make the long drive home.

I go into the house and lock the door, then head into the bathroom and turn on the tap in the shower. While I undress, I think about our walk on the beach. Thinking of Matt as I shower, I relive every moment of our star-filled evening.

Chapter Fifteen

Early the next morning, I write to Matt:

I've been wanting to ask you if we could save September 7th just for us, the twenty-fifth anniversary of the date we met. If I knew back then what I know now, I would have bewitched you and made you mine long ago. Sending love, Kaity.

Matt responds:

Getting together on September 7th sounds like a great way to celebrate that anniversary. I'm getting ready to head to the city for a doctor appointment, so I'll call you later. BTW, I like the bewitching part of your email A LOT! Sending love, Matt.

I reply:

I'm happy you like the bewitching part A LOT! But I think it's YOU who have bewitched ME! Sending love, Kaity.

~ * ~

An hour or so later, Matt calls to tell me he will pick me up to go to lunch after his doctor appointment. "I figure sometime around one o'clock. I'm thinking my appointment won't take too long because this doctor is usually very punctual, so it might be as early as noon. Will that work for you?"

"I'll be waiting," I tell him.

~ * ~

Matt picks me up at twelve-thirty. "How was your doctor appointment," I ask.

"I have some good news and some bad news. I'll explain over lunch."

"Nothing too bad, I hope."

"Nothing too terrible, but I'll let you be the judge when I tell you."

Since it's well before three o'clock, we have lunch at the coffee shop near my home. We both order cheeseburgers and Cokes.

"I have to have a special type of blood test," Matt tells me.

"What kind of blood test?"

"It's a test I have to have every year due to the loss of a kidney."

Holey Hell! "You lost a kidney?"

"I had a ten-pound cancerous tumor on a kidney, and the kidney had to be removed along with the tumor."

"Oh my gosh, Matt. I'm so sorry. Why didn't you mention it before?"

"There was no need. I function just fine with one kidney. I'm very healthy otherwise."

"So, what's the good news?" I ask.

"That is the good news. The bad news is I have to abstain from having sex for fourteen days before the test."

"Starting when?"

"Today," Matt answers. "Well, after today, no sex for fourteen days."

I look at my watch. "So, we have about eleven hours before the abstinence clock starts ticking, right?"

"Right," he says.

Our lunch arrives and Matt says, "Let's eat and run. We can beat the clock."

"Tick tock," I say.

We scarf down our lunches and head back to my house.

Chapter Sixteen

Matt and I arrive back at my house and go inside. We head to my bedroom and undress each other. Matt puts his arms around me, and I kiss him, tasting each corner of his mouth, and we tumble onto my bed. Our tongues join in a dance of their own, each of us trying to give more than the other. The passion swells in both of us when our bodies join, and my entire body shudders with an overpowering climax that rushes through me when Matt explodes within me.

We lie together after our lovemaking and Matt says, "If we would have connected when we were working together at age sixteen, Kaity, I could have been fucking you since then."

"I've been thinking that since we reconnected."

"If I'd have told you I wanted to fuck you in my first email," Matt says, "would you have told me to come on over?"

"Uh, no. Because I didn't know then what I know now, and I wouldn't even have known how to tell you."

"Here's another thought. If we'd have hooked up when I lived just a mile away from you, we might have been fucking for the past couple of years. Now we have to make up for lost time."

"Yes, now we do have to make up for lost time, and we've no more time to waste."

"Tick tock," Matt says, and kisses my neck. His hands grip my ass, and he slips his dick into me, pulling me tighter and closer to him, our arousal building together, higher and hotter, faster and frantic. My warm and wet combines with his hard and large, and our passion peaks. We hold one another as we climax together, our tongues entwined, our bodies joined in a sweltering moment of bliss.

Ann Moran

Languishing after our lovemaking, Matt asks, "When did you first fantasize about fucking me?"

He's asked me that before. I didn't admit then that it was when we were in our teens, and I won't admit it now. "I don't know when I started fantasizing about it, but lately I fantasize about it all the time. You've reminded me I'm very sexual."

"Get on your knees," he tells me.

"Tick tock, Matt," I say, and I drop to my knees.

~ * ~

It's a few minutes before midnight, and Matt's getting ready to leave. We embrace and kiss passionately. "I don't know how I'm going to survive the next two weeks without having sex with you," he tells me.

I agree. "I wish we could turn the clock back so we could make love once more so I could etch every wonderful moment into my memory and relive each and every one all the nights until we can make love again."

Matt looks at his watch. "We could pretend we're on the West Coast. It would give us two more hours."

I laugh. "It's a tempting idea, but I don't want us to mess up your blood test."

We kiss again, and Matt heads for home.

Chapter Seventeen

It's September 7th, the twenty-fifth anniversary of the day Matt and I met for the first time. Both of us dressed in jeans and T-shirts, we drive into the city, headed to the place where we met. We reminisce about those long-ago days when we were sixteen years old, and our futures were still before us. We reach into our memories and recall the names of the people with whom we worked all those years ago. This day is for memories of the way we were once upon a time.

We arrive at the old grocery store, which is now a Walgreen's, and sit for a minute in the parking lot, looking around before we exit the car. We hold hands as we walk and enter the store. We walk by what used to be the grocery store's customer service booth, past where the cash registers used to be, and make a left turn where the cigarette case once stood tall, sort of separating "upfront" from the rest of the store.

We turn to the right and can almost smell the delights of what had once been the bakery. We walk down the first aisle, where we remember our produce pal restocking lettuce and cabbage and peaches and plums. Along the back of the store was the butcher area, where the meat cases were filled with steaks and chops and ground beef. We remember the aisles and aisles of canned and packaged goods, tomato sauce and egg noodles, cookies, and bread.

We seek out the Walgreen's manager, tell him our story of how we met there twenty-five years ago, and receive permission to access the back of the store. We tour the area where the break room used to be, the dairy cooler, the meat locker, the freezer, the produce and dock areas, and we are filled with the nostalgic memories of our youth. I feel a lump in my throat and tears gathering behind my eyes, and I turn to kiss Matt's lips.

On our drive home, we talk about the special place we just visited. We talk about then, and we talk about now, reminding ourselves we will begin making up for our lost years in another week.

Before going home, we decide to have dinner at a favorite restaurant, and it's early evening when we arrive there. While enjoying our meal, we talk again about making up for lost time, and how much we are looking forward to getting together again next week after Matt's blood test. The date is written in indelible ink on my calendar.

Matt brings me home, and we wrap our arms around one another. We agree it was a good day and kiss good night.

Tomorrow will begin Year Twenty-Six.

Chapter Eighteen

We have one more day to go. I've written Matt naughty emails all week. Every day. Sometimes more than once a day, and each and every email is filled with my naughtiest fantasies, telling him all the things I want to do to him, and all the things I hope he will do to me. After his blood test, Matt will come over to my house, and hot sparks will fly.

Matt calls and says, "My cock is so hard thinking about fucking you."

"I'm getting wet just thinking about it. One more day."

"I want to video us having sex tomorrow," Matt says.

"It will be awesome to watch afterward. You just reminded me of a scene in a novel I read where a couple go to the beach and video themselves so they can go back to their hotel afterward and watch the video. I'm going to grab the book and read that scene tonight before bed."

"I hope you'll touch yourself while you read it, Kaity."

"Now there's an idea, but it'll make it difficult to turn the pages."

"Hmmm. I didn't think about you having sticky fingers and not being able to turn the pages. But get ready to be a porn star with me fucking you every imaginable way. Are you going to be ready for me tomorrow?"

"I'll be wet and ready."

"I'm heading to a meeting and probably won't get home until late. I'll write instead of calling, so I don't wake you. But I'm going to write and tell you everything I'm thinking about. Is that okay?"

"Of course, it's okay. Tomorrow, Matt."

Tomorrow is almost here, and it can't come quickly enough.

~ * ~

I wake up just past midnight and check my email to see if Matt has written. He has, and I read his words:

Let me begin by telling you I am hornier than hell, and I hope you won't find this email offensive. But after reading the emails you've been sending me all week; I think we're on the same page in terms of sexual fantasies.

Did you ever think you could enjoy getting fucked as much as I'm going to fuck you? You make my cock so hard I'm ready to explode. If I wasn't typing, I'd stroke myself right now.

When we get together tomorrow, I'm going to video us. We'll make our own collection of porn, and I want you to be as naughty as you've been in the emails you've been sending me. I don't want you holding back on anything. I want you talking as vulgar as you do in your emails.

I want you to tell me to take pictures of us having sex. I'll say spread your legs wide open, and I'm going to tell you to bend over so I can fuck you doggie style. I'm going to stop here before I explode.

Sweet dreams, Kaity. I hope you're dreaming of tomorrow. Sending love, Matt.

Wow and Holey Moley!
Tomorrow is today.

Chapter Nineteen

It's September 14th, and Matt calls me first thing in the morning. "My appointment is at ten-thirty, so see you soon."

"Can't wait," I respond.

~ * ~

Matt arrives at my house at noon. We head into my bedroom and quickly undress. "Are you going to video us?" I ask.

Matt picks up his cellphone. "Yes!"

I get on my knees, and Matt begins videoing. Knowing I'm on camera makes me very wet. Matt moans and tells me that he's almost ready to explode. He sits on my bed and tells me to straddle him, and then his cellphone focuses on me. I impale myself on his erection, and the orgasm that racks my body sends a new wave of wet that drenches me. Matt leans his cellphone against a pillow facing us and continues videoing. Then he pounds up and into me and seems to reach new heights. Our bodies shiver and shudder as we climax at the same time.

Matt closes his cellphone, and I fall into his arms. "I'm sleepy, Matt. I was awake most of the night after reading your email."

"Close your eyes, Kaity. A nap will do us both good before I take you to dinner. And then we can come back here afterward and watch our video."

~ * ~

Matt and I return to my house after dinner to watch our video. We hardly begin watching before we nearly tear off our clothes and are all over each other. We rock and roll and pump and pound, and we climax together again just as the video comes to its end.

Gasping for breath, I say, "Holey Moley, Matt. That was amazing."

"Fucking amazing." Matt says, and he gets dressed.

I slip into a robe and walk Matt to the door. We kiss, and then he leaves to make his long drive home.

~ * ~

Matt sends me an email when he gets home:

Whoa Nellie! That video was something else. I want to watch it again, but I'm going to try to hold off and wait until we can watch it together. Just thinking about that video is making me hard. It's unbelievable. What a fucking turn on. Sending love, Matt.

I respond:

You've awakened feelings in me I didn't know I had. And our video—OMG! Sending love, Kaity.

Matt replies:

I like the way you think, you naughty porn queen. See you tomorrow. I'm going to sign off now. Wishing you sweet dreams and sending love, Matt.

Chapter Twenty

It's the end of September, and the windows are open because the weather is still summerlike. I have a new work assignment, and I'm working in my home office, abstracting depositions, when Matt calls to say he's on his way. I mark my place and turn off my computer.

I go into the kitchen and open the refrigerator. I put together a chicken salad and make sandwiches in case Matt's hungry when he arrives. The way to a man's heart is—probably not chicken salad. I laugh. I wrap up the sandwiches in foil and put them in the fridge for snacking on later.

I take a quick shower and put my hair up in a ponytail. I dress in jeans and a Chicago Cubs T-shirt.

Matt arrives, and we embrace and kiss. "How was your day?" I ask.

"Ugh," is his response.

"That good, huh?"

"I always have so much to do I can't seem to get abreast of it all. Speaking of getting a breast"—his hand goes under my T-shirt, and his fingers tweak a boob— "maybe I can get a breast after all."

"Oooh," I say. "That was rather nice. My other boob is jealous."

Matt lifts my T-shirt over my head and tosses it onto a chair. He touches my breasts with his fingers, then sucks one nipple into his mouth and then the other. And I feel the wet begin.

"Are you hungry?" I ask.

"For you, yes. Very hungry. I've been thinking about fucking you all day." Matt tugs on my ponytail and says, "Let's go to your room and get naked."

~ * ~

After making love, Matt says, "Now I'm hungry for food."

"I made chicken salad sandwiches."

Matt leans over and kisses me. "Sounds good. I hope you won't mind if I take it with me to eat on the road. I've got another heavy day tomorrow, and I should get going."

While we get dressed, I say, "You're welcome to stay, Matt."

"Thanks, but I have an early start tomorrow, and there's always the prep work I have to do."

Dressed again, we go into the kitchen. I give a sandwich to Matt and walk him to the front door.

"We were awesome tonight," I say.

"Fucking awesome," Matt agrees.

We embrace. "Drive safe."

"Always," he says, and kisses me good night.

I close and lock the door behind him and go into the kitchen. I eat my own sandwich, wishing Matt would've stayed.

Chapter Twenty-One

I head to downtown Chicago on a lovely autumn morning. I wear a black pin-striped slack suit and don't need a coat on this sixty-degree day. I board a Metra train with about a dozen other commuters riding into the city and arrive at Union Station just before ten-thirty.

My trial bag is heavy, laden with the deposition binders I prepared. The law firm of Williams, Anderson & Mason is located in the American Medical Association—AMA—building in the River North District at the far north end of the Loop. Which means it's quite a hike from Union Station. It's a nice refreshing walk on good weather days like today. However, carrying the heavy trial bag along with my briefcase will make walking that distance difficult, so I opt to cab it to the office instead.

The taxi drops me off on the Wabash Avenue side of the AMA building. I get into an elevator and ride up to the law firm on the thirtieth floor. I haven't been to the office since August when I was here to prep with the team for the previous trial in Boston, and I wave to familiar faces as I make my way to my office.

I unpack the trial bag and call Zach Eberle, the attorney in charge of the case I'm working on. I don't have to identify myself because my name will appear in the Caller ID section of Zach's telephone. "Hi, Zach, I'm just letting you know I'm here."

"Right on time," he says. "We're meeting in Conference Room A on the twenty-eighth floor. I'll meet you there."

I repack the trial bag and lug it with me down to the twenty-eighth floor. I wave a hello to Maisy, the receptionist, and make my way to the conference room. I pull open the heavy door and go inside.

Zach is already there, writing on a legal pad.

"Hey, Zach," I say.

He stands to greet me and takes the heavy trial bag from me and places it on the table. "It's good to see you, Kaity."

He's tall and slender with a square jaw and has hazel eyes with long dark lashes. He has coppery red hair with a slight curl, and a few curls fall onto his forehead. He's sort of a taller version of Sonny Corleone, and his cologne smells wonderful. He's probably somewhere in his forties, and a romance writer might describe him as ruggedly handsome. Zach is a successful litigator and a hunk, and I can't help wondering if his good looks have contributed to any of his many courtroom victories.

He helps me unload the trial bag, and we place the binders on the conference room table. "Help yourself to lunch," he tells me. "The rest of the team will be here shortly." And then he goes back to writing.

Lunch has already been set out on the buffet table, and I fill a plate and take a seat at the table. The rest of the team arrives. They get their lunches and take their seats at the table as well. When everyone is situated, the meeting begins.

~ * ~

Zach accompanies me back to my office when the meeting ends. I sit down behind my desk, and he closes the door. "You did an excellent job on that spreadsheet," he says. "Do you mind taking a few minutes to explain to me exactly how it works?"

I turn on my computer and bring up the spreadsheet. Zach stands behind me, looking over my shoulder at the computer screen the way an umpire stands behind a baseball catcher, and I inhale his scent.

"Okay, all you have to do is type whatever you're looking for into this search field"—I move the cursor to the search field— "and then Click. Anything even remotely relevant to our case will come up—the districts, the courts, the judges, the plaintiffs, the defendants, conclusions, affirmations, dissenting opinions, class actions," I rattle off excitedly. I look back at Zach and see that he's smiling. "You'll get whatever you're looking for. Search it, and it will all come up in the column on the far right," I say and point to the column.

"That's amazing, Kaity," he says and puts a hand on my shoulder, "and it will be extremely useful. Thank you."

Zach goes back around to the other side of my desk, sits down and crosses his long legs, making himself comfortable in one of my visitor chairs. "I hope it's okay for me to tell you that you look great. You must be living right."

"Thanks." He would not believe how right I'm living, and I feel myself blush. Zach also looks great, dressed today in a Georgio Armani suit, the varying hues of the fabric's light greens softly blended and parlayed into an unobtrusive plaid. His shirt has a soft green cast to it, and his tie, definitely pure silk, is beige with varying shades of green specks that complement the color of his suit. As far as Zach is concerned, looking great is an understatement. Terrific would be more accurate. "You look terrific," I tell him, and wish I knew what kind of cologne he uses because the scent is phenomenal.

Zach smiles and says, "Thank you."

"Back to Boston in early December," I say.

"Yes, and we've got a lot of work to do to get ready."

Zach is the ultimate planner, and trial preparation for Zach encompasses a lengthy and highly detailed list of the work he wants done.

"The judge has blocked two weeks for trial," he says. "I don't believe we'll need that long, but in any event, we'll be back before the holidays."

But the team will be headed to Boston to prep after Thanksgiving, which means I will be away from Matt for more than three weeks. Longer even than the two weeks we had to abstain from having sex before his blood test.

"You're going to need to review the rest of the documents in order to prepare the reports I need," Zach says.

His assistant, Abby Dixon, will be able to gather whatever I need. "I'll touch base with Abby and ask her to FedEx to me the documents I need."

"Good enough," he says. "Any questions?"

Yes, how will I survive more than three weeks without Matt? "No, I think you covered everything in the meeting."

"Feel free to call me if something comes to mind," Zach says and stands.

I stand as well. "Unless you need me for something else, I'm going to head home."

"As a matter of fact, do you have time to have a drink with me? Get out of here and give us a chance to catch up a bit?"

We've known each other for years and have always been friendly with one another, but this is new and seems to be a step up from friendly. But hey. "Of course."

"How about Travelle?"

The restaurant/bar in the Langdon Hotel is located at the opposite end of the same building in which WAM is located. "Sounds good to me," I say.

He opens the door. "Come on," he says, extending a hand to indicate I should precede him out of my office. "Beauty before age."

I grab my briefcase and exit my office ahead of him. Is it my imagination or is Zach acting kind of weird? We walk up the corridor and nod to several people we encounter as we make our way to the elevator vestibule. Zach presses the down button, and we enter the elevator when the doors open.

~ * ~

The elevator arrives in the lobby, and we walk to the southern end of the building. We enter the Langham lobby and take an elevator to the second floor. Arriving at Travelle, we sit down at a small table overlooking the plaza, and I set down my briefcase. We have a nice view of the surrounding area—Wacker Drive straight ahead to the south, with State Street to the west and Wabash Avenue to the east. A server stops by, and we both order Bloody Marys.

"So, what's going on in your life?" Zach asks.

"Nothing too much. I work a lot of hours."

Zach smiles and says, "Yes, you do. You've got a mean old boss."

I smile back and say, "Not true. My boss is terrific and works much harder than I do."

"I appreciate you saying that. After this trial, things likely will slow down somewhat due to the holidays."

Our drinks arrive and I raise my glass. "To taking time to smell the roses." We touch glasses and sip our drinks. "I don't know anybody who works harder than you do, Zach. But are you having any fun? Taking time to relax?"

"I admit I may be a bit of a workaholic, but I love my work, as I believe you know."

A lot more than a bit, but at least he's aware he probably works too hard. "I do know, and you're one hell of a good lawyer, Zach. I'm proud to work with you." I lift my glass once more and say, "A toast to excellence," and I touch my glass to Zach's again.

"I'll drink to that," he smiles and says, and we both sip our drinks. "Thanks, Kaity. That was very nice."

"I speak the truth but remember—all work and no play makes Zach a dull boy."

"I believe the dull boy's name is Jack," he says and smiles.

"Right you are. And Jack needs to be careful he doesn't end up sad and gray."

"I hope you won't tell me what to do when life gives me lemons."

"My only advice would be to make Lemon Margaritas," I say.

We laugh together and sip our cocktails.

"Seriously, Zach, are you taking time to relax? What are you doing for fun?"

"I'm having fun right now, having a drink with you and being entertained with your simple words of wisdom."

I smile.

"You look terrific, Kaity, so something must be going right in your life."

"Nothing too exciting," I say. But that isn't true. What's going right in my life is very exciting, and I wonder why I'm holding back from telling Zach about Matt.

"Well, I'd like to have some of whatever it is you're smoking because whatever's going on with you has put the kind of smile on your face that I haven't seen in quite some time. And I'd like to drink to that."

We lift and touch glasses and toast once again.

We finish our drinks, and Zach leaves cash on the table. I pick up my briefcase, and we leave Travelle and walk back to the northern elevator bank at the other end of the building. Before getting on an elevator, Zach says, "Call me if you need anything, Kaity," and he winks. "Anything at all."

I nod and go out to the taxi line to get a cab to take me to Union Station for my train ride home. Did Zach just wink at me, or did I imagine that he did? And I wonder again why I didn't tell him about Matt.

~ * ~

It's midafternoon when I arrive home. After dropping off my briefcase in my home office, I go into my bedroom and undress. I head to the bathroom to shower, then slip into my robe after toweling off. While I dry my hair, I think about Zach and wonder once more if my imagination has run rampant. And I think of Matt and wonder again why I didn't tell Zach about him. I seem to be doing a lot of wondering again lately.

I hope Matt is still planning to stop off on his way to somewhere or other. I hardly have the thought when he calls.

"Hey, Kaity. I have to attend a meeting late tonight, but we could spend a couple of hours together if you wouldn't mind meeting me at LN1."

LN1 is the code name for Love Nest 1, what we call the hotel we'd gone to our first time. It was my corny suggestion when I was feeling all warm and fuzzy. Matt laughed when I proposed the name, but it's now our own private joke. "Don't you want to come to my house?"

"I'm only about twenty minutes away from the hotel, so if you would meet me there, we'd have more time to spend together. Take an Uber to the hotel now, and I'll drop you off at home on my way to the meeting."

"Sure. I'll see you soon."

I call for an Uber and dress in comfy jeans and a green paisley top. I twist my hair into a knot and pin it atop my head. I choose gold heart earrings and spritz myself with Opium. I grab my jacket from the front hall closet when my Uber arrives, and I'm on my way.

~ * ~

Matt is waiting for me when I arrive at LN1, and he hugs me tightly to him. He's already checked in, and we make our way up the corridor to the elevator. The elevator door closes, and we kiss passionately as the elevator ascends. Arriving on the third floor, we head down the corridor to our room. Matt opens the door, and I follow him inside.

We undress each other and sit on the bed. I sit with my legs tucked beneath me, and Matt sits beside me. I lean over to kiss him.

"Do you want to watch our video?" he asks.

"Yes!" I answer.

Matt opens his cellphone, and the video begins to play. "Kaity, sit on my lap," he says, and I wrap Matt in a warm embrace, meeting his lips in a deep tongue-sharing kiss as I lower myself onto his erection. Watching the video makes us both hotter, and we pull out all the stops. Almost there, we moan together, and then we are there, hot spurts of his ejaculation shooting up into me, and waves of my wet raining down on him to put out the fire in his loins.

"Fucking awesome," Matt says. "You and our video."

It's time to leave, and we dress and leave LN1. Matt drives me home and walks me to my door. We kiss good night, and Matt gets back in his car to drive to his meeting.

Chapter Twenty-Two

It's the last Saturday in October, a crisp and sunny afternoon, as Matt and I crunch colorful leaves beneath our feet while completing a run. We arrive back at my house, winded but energized, and treat ourselves to bottles of water from my fridge.

"Shower?" I suggest.

Matt finishes his water and nods. "Race you there."

We arrive at the same time, quickly undress, and get into the shower. We soap each other up and make love in the shower while the water pummels our bodies. After rinsing off, Matt turns off the shower tap. We get out of the shower and towel each other off.

After getting dressed, we go into the kitchen. "I have a meeting in a few hours," Matt says, "so I should get going."

"Do you have time to eat before you go? There's leftover chicken in the fridge."

"That sounds good," he says.

While he scrounges the refrigerator searching for the leftover piece of blackened chicken I cooked the night before, I take an apple from the bowl of fruit on my kitchen table. I sit down in a chair and bite into the Honeycrisp, enjoying its sweet-but-tangy flavor.

Matt finds the chicken and puts it on a plate to heat in the microwave. He joins me at the table to eat his chicken. When he's finished eating, he runs his hands under water from the kitchen faucet and wipes his hands on a paper towel. He stands behind me and bends to kiss the top of my head. "The chicken was really tasty. Thanks."

I walk him to the front door. We embrace and kiss, and Matt goes on his way.

Chapter Twenty-Three

It's early November, and I'm in my office working from home. I finish another report Zach Eberle requested, make a file folder label and insert the report into the folder.

It's nearly four o'clock, and I decide to go for my run before darkness falls and night settles in. I turn off my computer, change into running clothes and slip into my sneakers.

I think I smell snow in the air as I run my usual mile and head back home under a darkening sky. I hear the house phone ringing as I walk in the door and hurry to answer, thinking it's probably Matt calling.

"Hey," I say.

"Hey yourself," Zach says. "How's it going?"

Darn. I was hoping it was Matt calling to say he was on his way, but back to Zach. "Good. I finished my case summaries today and filled an entire banker's box with everything you requested. FedEx picked it up, so you'll have everything tomorrow morning."

"Thanks for the heads up," he says. "The reason I'm calling, though, is to ask if you'd be available for a meeting next week so I can make assignments for putting the finishing touches on the trial documents."

This is unusual. Zach's assistant, Abby Dixon, is the one who usually calls to set up meetings.

"Sure, which day next week?"

"I'm thinking Friday at eleven o'clock, and we'll order in lunch. Depending on how much we accomplish on Friday will determine whether we'll need a follow-up meeting the following week."

"Friday's fine. I'll see you then."

"Abby is making calls to the rest of the team, so I'll let you know if we have to move the meeting to another day."

Holey Moley. Abby is calling the other team members, but Zach called me. This is getting curiouser and curiouser.

"One more thing, Kaity. Let's plan to have a drink after the meeting."

He disconnects the call before I can respond. Which is just as well because I have no idea what I'd say. Has my imagination gone into overdrive again? Before I can give it another thought, the phone rings again.

I answer the phone, and this time the caller is Matt. "I'm on my way," he says.

"I can't wait to see you."

~ * ~

Matt arrives, and we go into my bedroom. We undress and crawl into bed. We make love, but he seems distracted, and our lovemaking is not as passionate as it usually is. I lay my head on Matt's chest. "Is everything okay?"

He sits up and says, "I've got a lot on my mind and too much to do."

I want to make love again—undistracted this time. I sit up beside him and put my arms around his neck. I kiss him and say, "You need to relax, Matt, and I have a good idea of how to relax you." I reach between his legs to touch him and lower my head.

He moves both my hand and head away and says, "I have to get going." He gets up and gathers his clothing to get dressed.

Something is wrong, and I want to have a chance to fix whatever it is. "Please tell me you'll stay tonight."

"I've got to make another early start tomorrow, and I have several meetings I have to prepare for tonight."

"Will you ever be able spend the night with me?"

As he dresses, he says, "You know how busy I am. I've made no secret of it. It's best I'm home in the morning to get a good start on the day."

I don't want him to leave when I feel that something is wrong. If he can't stay with me, then I'll go home with him. Determined to fix whatever it is that's bothering him, I say, "I'll go home with you. I'll bring my laptop and work from your house."

"That won't work because I don't know when I'd be able to bring you back here."

I pull on jeans and a sweatshirt and put on my running shoes and tie the laces. I stand up. "If we can't get back here for a couple of days, no sweat. I'm working from home, so it doesn't matter where I work. I'll just grab a change of clothing or two, and I'll be set to go."

I open my closet door, grab my duffel bag, and put a couple pairs of jeans and a few T-shirts inside. I open a dresser drawer and pick out underwear. I grab socks and add all the items to the duffel.

"Stop, Kaity. Taking you home with me isn't a good idea."

"What does that mean?" I stop what I'm doing when something like ice water sluices through my veins. "Matt, is your Traveling Partner still living with you?"

"Regardless of what my relationship is with her, I don't want to be murdered while I sleep."

"You ended your relationship *six months ago*, Matt. What the hell?"

He's dressed and puts his jacket on. He comes to me and puts his arms around me. "Kaity, it's complicated, but there's nothing to be upset about. I have to go."

I cross my arms over my chest and look away. Matt kisses the top of my head and heads out the door.

~ * ~

After Matt leaves, I think about our conversation. He's always been honest and upfront about stuff, and I wonder why I'm doubting him now. Why? Because it's been *six long months* since he ended his relationship with his Traveling Partner. That's why. *Six months.* Come on, if there's nothing to it, why didn't he mention that she's still living with him?

But I feel bad for the way I let the evening end. I didn't even kiss him good night. Since Thanksgiving is a few weeks away, I decide to email him and invite him for Thanksgiving dinner. I begin my email:

Would you like to have Thanksgiving dinner with me? I'll cook a turkey and stuffing and all the trimmings.

My folks will be disappointed that I won't be having Thanksgiving dinner with them, but I'll explain the situation and make them understand.

I continue my email to Matt:

We still have so much to talk about, and we could spend the day talking, eating, fucking, talking, watching football, napping, talking, snacking, and fucking again. I'm so thankful to have you in my life, and it would be wonderful to share Thanksgiving with you. Sending love, Kaity.

Matt calls a couple of hours later. "Spending Thanksgiving together would be nice. However, I'm going to be in Arkansas."

"You'll be in Arkansas for Thanksgiving?"

"Yes, I'll be spelunking, exploring and treasure hunting with the guys for a week or more. We probably won't get back until the beginning of December. We're going to try to find this huge old cave one of the guys found many years ago."

He's going to Arkansas and didn't even mention he's going away. I wonder if his Traveling Partner will be traveling with him to Arkansas, but I bite my tongue. I have no hold on him. We exchange good nights and end our conversation.

If there's any good news, I think as I hang up the phone, it's that I won't have to do any explaining to my folks after all.

Chapter Twenty-Four

It's several days later, and there's no word from Matt. He always responds to my naughty emails, though, so I sit down and write him one using every naughty word I can think of.

He responds:

Is having sex all you think about?

His response chills me. He used to love my naughty talk. Hell, he *taught* me to talk naughty. And we've been making love—fucking our brains out! —several times a week, sometimes twice the same day. It makes no sense at all that he sent me this kind of response.

We haven't spent any time together in days. We've gone from phone calls and emailing and texting sometimes ten times a day to almost nothing. Something has changed, and I email Matt again to ask him about it:

I realize you are and have been very busy, and I've tried to respect that. We agreed we could tell each other anything and everything. With that in mind, I need to tell you about some stuff that's weighing on my mind.

And I go on to tell him what's on my mind:

I want and need you in my life. If companionship or friendship is all you have to offer, I told you I would accept any part of you that you are willing to share with me. I have so much more I want to share with you, whether we are friends or lovers. But I don't want to fool myself, and I need to know where I stand in your life.

~ * ~

I get a response from Matt:

My life is topsy-turvy right now, and I'm running nonstop. Last night I got a call at midnight and had to leave the house to resolve a crisis. I was awakened at seven o'clock this morning by a call from a frantic client, and it took several hours for me to calm him down and assure him things weren't as bad as he was projecting. This is just another day in my life.

I had another meeting at six this evening. I just got home and it's after midnight. I have to attend a neighbor's funeral tomorrow and then deal with the other things on my schedule. Wednesday and Thursday I have to help a buddy move stuff from his fire-damaged home to his new one. Since he was storing some stuff for me, I have no choice but to help him. I have meetings all day on Friday and another one on Saturday.

I've been so busy I haven't had time for us, and the one thing you can't lose sight of is that I'm still in a relationship with my Traveling Partner despite what I told you. We own a lot of property together. which makes things difficult.

So, he *is* still in some kind of relationship with his Traveling Partner, which doesn't bode well for our relationship. I pause for a moment before continuing to read his response:

Nothing has changed, but I don't want to mislead you when even I don't know in what direction I'm headed because there's so much on my plate. I thought it would get easier, but I've been even busier than I was before. I don't want to lose you because I can't fill all the roles you may expect of me.

What roles did I ask him to fill? I reply:

I don't expect you to fill any roles. I never did and never will. I just hope we can be part of each other's lives in any way we can be.

Matt writes:

I'm glad you understand my situation and can live with it. I just have so many obligations to so many people. It's often complicated. Here we are, two people, where one of us influenced greatly the life of the other. That influence has been appreciated ever since by me, the recipient of your influence, and it was important enough that I had to search you out to say thank you. If that thank you opened other doors for us, it's a bonus for which we should be grateful.

I sigh. The truth of the matter is that I don't understand his situation at all. Nor do I want to deal with him being in any kind of lingering relationship with his Traveling Partner. It's time for me to rethink things because the bonus he mentioned isn't making me feel the least bit grateful.

Chapter Twenty-Five

Matt calls me several days later. "Something has been wrong with my email account. I keep having problems opening it. It's been going on for days, so if I'm late in responding to your emails, that's the reason."

"Thanks for letting me know." Hoping there's a chance to revive our floundering relationship, I ask, "Would you be interested in a post-Thanksgiving dinner when you return from Arkansas?"

"I would love to say yes, but I cannot commit to anything because I don't even know what will be happening an hour from now."

"There's no reason to commit to anything," I say. "If it works out, then we'll do it. We'll plan the best we can."

"I appreciate that you understand this and ask that you don't lose sight of how you put that into a simple perspective. I'll do what I can to keep us together, but I cannot commit to anything. Keep in mind that others absolutely WILL NOT understand the relationship we are developing, so don't let them sway you in any direction. I don't need someone coming in and upsetting the apple cart with their conventional wisdom. Our relationship goes back decades, and most people are incapable of understanding that. We know what we're dealing with, and that should be all that matters."

"You told me I shouldn't lose sight of the fact that you're still in a relationship with your Traveling Partner despite what you told her," I remind him. "Does that mean you're still in an intimate relationship with her?"

"I don't know what kind of relationship I have right now because I'm way too busy to be intimate, and it's not like she's breaking the door down to be either."

This does not sound reassuring. Something is terribly amiss. It's been well over a week since we spent any time together, and Matt seems to be backing away. I scold myself for being so pathetic and wonder if I'm simply naive or whether I'm just plain fucking stupid.

Chapter Twenty-Six

I choose a long-sleeve sweater dress of a soft blue color for the trial team's luncheon meeting. I wear small hoop earrings and my gold Timex. It's crisp and cold this mid-November morning, and I slip my arms into the sleeves of my parka. I call for an Uber to take me to the Metra train station and grab my briefcase.

I arrive downtown a half hour before the meeting is scheduled to begin and walk from Union Station to the AMA building. I take the elevator to the thirtieth floor and arrive in the office of WAM a few minutes before the start of the meeting. I go to my office and hang up my parka, then head down to the twenty-eighth floor.

I greet Maisy, the receptionist, and walk down the corridor to Conference Room A. Lunch has been delivered and Abby Dixon, Zach's assistant, is unpacking various containers of food containing chicken and roast beef, tofu, potato and green salads, various flavors of yogurts, as well as cookies and brownies, and she places the platters of food on the buffet table at the rear of the conference room. "Hi Abby," I say. "It's nice to see you."

"It's good to see you too, Kaity," she says.

I notice that the blonde and blue-eyed Abby is sporting a large sparkling diamond on her ring finger. "Whoa, Abby. Your ring is beautiful! Let me have a better look."

Abby holds up her hand to show off the brilliant Marquise diamond sitting atop a simple band of gold.

"My gosh, how many carats is it?" I ask.

"Almost two," Abby answers.

"It's dazzling," I tell her and smile.

"Do you like it?" she asks.

"I love it. It's the most beautiful ring I've ever seen. Did you choose it?"

"No, he did," Abby tells me.

"He has wonderful taste," I say and give Abby a hug. "It's truly magnificent. Congratulations! Did you and Evan get back together again?"

"No, that was a mistake that I try not to think about anymore."

"Sorry, Abby."

"No worries, Kaity. But let me tell you about Tom. We met when we were in high school. He was my first love, and we've been having a lot of fun getting reacquainted."

"I'm happy for you, Abby. I also met the guy I've been seeing during our high school years. He contacted me out of the blue a couple of months ago."

"So, you're seeing someone," Abby says.

"I was, but I'm no longer sure. I think he may be backing away from our relationship. I thought he might be The One, but he's suddenly not certain what direction he wants his life to take."

Abby continues setting out the platters of food. "Let me give you a hand," I offer, and pitch in to help. "It looks like a lot of food for eight people."

"I ordered for twelve," Abby says. "I like to be sure we have enough in case Zach invites others to our meeting. You know Zach. Prepare for every contingency."

"You're right about that, but it's why he's such a terrific lawyer. He's the epitome of excellence. A true perfectionist."

"He is that" Abby agrees. "And we never have to worry about any food going to waste because we'll have the leftovers sent up to the kitchen. You know how people love it when there's free food in the kitchen."

I laugh. "Yes, because I'm one of those people."

A couple members of the trial team arrive—Michael Cole, my paralegal counterpart, and Maria Shue, the other team secretary who is Abby's counterpart—and they greet us and head for the buffet table.

"Thanks for your help, Kaity. I saved you a seat next to mine. Let's get our lunch before all the good food is gone."

Abby and I fill our plates and take seats at the table Abby indicates. A few minutes later, Jason Whitely, Stefanie Jones and Gregory Norris—the litigation associate team members—arrive, greet the rest of the team and serve themselves at the buffet table.

"Sorry to hear your boyfriend is backing away," Abby tells me.

"Thanks, Abby."

"But it will be good news for Zach," Abby says.

Huh? "What do you mean?"

"Zach will be down in a bit, Kaity. I'm going to let him know you're here." Abby smiles. "He's anxious to see you."

What the hell? "Wait, Abby. Hold on a second. What do you mean he's anxious to see me?"

Abby smiles and waves as she leaves the conference room, and I move over to sit with Michael and Maria.

Zach Eberle arrives five minutes later, looking especially Sonny-Corleoneish this morning. His suit is a dark blue Armani and a beautiful contrast to his coppery hair. His shirt is a lighter shade of blue, and his tie is grey with flecks of the same deep blue that color his suit. He's very tall and one heck of a handsome guy.

Zach greets the team and says, "It's good to see all of you. Enjoy lunch, and we'll get started shortly."

A moment later, he stands behind me. He leans down close to my ear and whispers, "You look wonderful. Don't forget we have a date for a cocktail when we're through here."

Holey Moley. I'd forgotten about that. But he smells really good. I inhale. Was it Vuitton? I smile up at him and say, "I'm looking forward to it."

"I was hoping you'd have chosen a seat closer to the head of the table, which is where I'm headed." He puts his hand on my shoulder and gives it a squeeze, then goes to the head of the table and takes his seat, anxious to start the meeting.

No way is this my imagination.

~ * ~

The meeting ends at five-thirty, and team members leave with their new assignments. I go back to my office, and Zach raps his knuckles against my name plate on the outside of my office a moment later. "I love your name plate," he says.

This is more than curious. It's downright peculiar, and I can't think of how to respond.

Zach is wearing his topcoat, obviously set to leave. "Ready?" he asks.

I remove my parka from the hook I'd hung it on, and Zach reaches for it and holds it while I put my arms into its sleeves.

I pick up my briefcase and Zach says, "Leave it. We'll come back and retrieve our briefcases later."

I put down my briefcase, and Zach gestures that I should precede him out of my office. We walk up the corridor together, wishing good nights and wishes for a good weekend to the attorneys and staff we encounter as we make our way to the elevator vestibule.

The elevator arrives, and there's nobody inside. The doors close, and we'll express to the Lobby unless the call button is pressed on the twenty-eighth or twenty-ninth floors. The elevator begins its descent without stopping and is on its way to the Lobby.

Zach puts an arm around my shoulders. "Thanks for agreeing to have a drink with me, Kaity. There's something I'd like to discuss with you, talk to you about."

I look up at him and see that his hazel eyes are like lazers, boring into my own. I don't know what to say. He apparently reads my mind and says, "Don't say anything until you hear what I have to say, okay?"

Not saying anything, at least not saying anything of substance, will not be a problem. "Okay, I guess." But he sure does smell good, and I inhale his scent. And he's so incredibly handsome.

"That's all I ask," he says and removes his arm from my shoulders when the elevator reaches the Lobby.

We exit the elevator and walk across State Street to the Tortoise Club.

Chapter Twenty-Seven

Zach holds the door for me, and we enter the Tortoise Club. We are greeted with smiles by a warm and welcoming staff and asked if we are there to dine or just want to have a drink while we listen to music in the lounge.

Zach turns to me and raises an inquiring eyebrow. "Kaity?"

"Just a drink."

We stop to check our coats, and Zach leads the way to the lounge. Happy hour is underway, and a live band plays soft jazz. Zach and I take seats at a small table in the bar area. He holds a chair out for me, and I sit. The atmosphere is cozy and intimate and somewhat old-fashioned, similar to what one might expect a classy restaurant to look like in an old black-and-white movie.

A waiter appears dressed in a white-collared shirt and black bow tie. I ask for a glass of Zinfandel, and Zach orders a Scotch on the rocks. The waiter is off to fetch our drinks, and Zach says, "So, Kaity, you must be wondering what this is all about, and I apologize if I've been mysterious."

To say the least.

"First off, I'd like to take this outside the office. It has nothing to do with the firm or our working together. And I don't want you to feel any pressure whatsoever. That's very important. I'm hoping you'll be willing to pretend it's a coincidence we both walked in here tonight and decided to have a drink together. Is that okay with you?"

He's making me nervous. "Zach, just please tell me what's on your mind."

"Sorry. It's just that I hardly know where to begin. I suppose the beginning is as good as any place to begin, so I'll begin at the beginning."

Zach is always articulate and well-spoken, but he now seems to be having difficulty putting together a meaningful sentence.

The waiter arrives with our drinks, and Zach takes a large swallow of his Scotch. I sip my Zinfandel and wait for Zach to go on.

"I know you've been married and divorced twice."

I sip my wine again. So even Zach knows I'm a two-time loser.

Zach takes another large swallow of his Scotch. "I understand you're currently involved with someone."

Am I? I'm not sure anymore, but I'm not ready to give up on Matt just yet. I take another sip of wine and say, "I've been seeing someone for several months now."

"Several months," he mutters softly. "Is it serious? Your relationship. What I mean is, uh, do you consider your relationship to be a serious one?"

Why is it any of Zach's business whether or not I'm in a relationship, regardless of whether or not it's serious? And what's up with him? Muttering? And he seems to be almost stumbling over words.

"I'm very—how should I say this? —interested," he says and takes a big sip of his Scotch, "so how serious is it?"

Holey Moley. I've heard speak Zach hundreds of times and the silver-tongued orator with whom I'm so familiar is nowhere near the top of his game tonight. He seems tense or maybe nervous about something.

I sip my wine to stall for time while I decide how I want to answer Zach. Until a couple of weeks ago, I thought the relationship Matt and I were building was very serious. I'd been thinking and hoping that we had a real shot at growing old together. Now I'm not sure if we have any kind of relationship. But how to answer Zach? And why is he asking? I decide to be vague, ambiguous, until I hear what more he has to say. "I think it might be," I say and sip my wine again. "Serious, I mean."

"Perhaps it would be best for me to hold off on this discussion before I embarrass myself."

What the hell is going on? I chug the rest of my wine, and Zach downs his Scotch.

"Would you like another glass of wine?" he asks.

I look at my watch and see that it's six-fifteen. I have to go back to the office to get my briefcase. If I leave now, I can get my briefcase, grab an Uber to the Metra station and catch the six-fifty train. I don't want to offend Zach, but I probably should decline and get going. "Thanks, Zach, but I have a long commute. I probably should get going."

"Have another glass of wine, Kaity, and enjoy the jazz. I'm happy to drive you home later."

"Okay, but then I'd like you to tell me what's on your mind."

"Deal," he says, and signals for the waiter to bring us fresh drinks.

Chapter Twenty-Eight

Zach rakes a hand through his coppery hair. "I want to apologize again, Kaity, for what surely must seem to you to be outlandish behavior."

He pauses when the waiter returns with our drinks, and then continues. "You were already working at the firm—what was it? Twenty-some years ago? —when I came on as a new associate right out of law school. Remember?" Zach takes a sip of his fresh Scotch.

"I do remember." I sip my wine. "It was twenty-three years ago. I worked days as a secretary and took night classes at the Junior College."

"Back then, your Kaitlyn Kinney name plate was affixed to the outside of your cubicle."

"Yes, and I signed up for De Paul's paralegal program and got my paralegal certificate a couple of years later."

Zach sips his Scotch. "I remember."

"It was a good move for me," I say, and take another sip of my wine.

"It was also a good move for me. For the firm, I mean. And I've always loved your name plate."

Peculiar may not be a strong enough word to describe the way Zach is acting. And what is his fascination with my name plate? "That same name plate is now affixed to the outside of my office."

He sips his Scotch and says, "Yours is a name I love."

"Which name? Kaitlyn or Kinney?"

"Both."

Maybe that explains why he knuckle rapped my name plate when he stopped at my office to pick me up. But there's no "maybe" about this conversation. It's bizarre.

"You obviously kept your maiden name."

83

Since he's fixated on my name plate, I decide to have some fun with him. "I didn't want to have to get a different name plate."

Zach smiles, and I sip my wine.

He takes a long drink of his Scotch then, and sort of laughs. "This probably will sound ridiculous and no doubt very 'high school,' but I don't know any other way to say it. I fell in like with you a long time ago, Kaity. I felt an immediate attraction to you the first time we met. It was 'like at first sight.' Or maybe it was lust. Nope, it was 'like at first sight.'"

Holy Shit! I pick up my wine glass and chug.

"There was a time when I thought you might have had some feelings more than friendship for me, too. It took me a year to work up the nerve to ask you out. And just when I'd worked up the courage to ask you for a date, I learned you'd gotten engaged."

Wow! Zach and I have been friendly with one another from the start, but I never thought it was anything more than friendship. I had no idea that he was interested in dating me.

Zach downs his Scotch and signals the waiter that we're ready for another round. "Shortly thereafter, I transferred to our Boston office. I returned to Chicago six years ago and discovered then that you'd left the firm the month before and moved to San Francisco."

Our drinks arrive, and we both take long sips.

"Abby told me you'd gotten divorced several years before and then met a guy online, and that meeting him was the reason for your move to San Francisco." Zach sighs. "I chided myself for not having kept in touch with you. You can't imagine how happy I was when you returned to the firm."

Zach sips his drink. "We've been working together again for about two years now, and it's taken all of that time for me, once again, to build up the courage to ask you out."

He lifts his glass and takes another swallow of his Scotch, and he sighs again. "I've never had a problem getting dates. I've dated a lot of women, and I'm fearless—almost audacious—when it comes to dating, so I don't know why you have this effect on me. I'm forty-six years old, Kaity, and I've never been in love. Can you believe that?" He sort of laughs again. "As I said, I've gone out with many women, but you're the first and only woman I've ever had feelings for, real feelings, I mean."

Holey Moley! Why is he telling me this stuff?

"You're my best writer and researcher, and I don't want to live without you for that reason alone." He smiles. "I have more confidence in your abilities than I do in some of our associates."

Back on more solid ground, I remind him, "Thanks, Zach, but I thought we were leaving this out of the office."

"Thanks for the reminder." Zach picks up his glass and touches it to mine "Let's drink to that."

I raise my wine glass, and we both sip our drinks.

"You are so sensual, Kaity. But you don't seem to be aware of it, which makes you even more sensual. Sexuality emanates from you the way sonar releases waves of sound seeking objects in the ocean. Pings."

If that's true, it isn't working on Matt lately.

Zach sips his drink again, and his glass is nearly empty. "I asked Abby today to find out if you were involved with anyone. I should have asked you myself when we had drinks a few weeks ago, so shame on me."

I suddenly remember that I held back from telling Zach about Matt that afternoon, and I wonder again why I didn't tell him.

"Abby thought the guy you were dating was backing away from your relationship, and she didn't think you were dating anybody else, at least not yet."

Zach's glass is empty. "Another?" he asks.

I finish my wine and nod my head, and Zach signals the waiter again. "So how long have you been in your relationship?" he asks.

"We met more than twenty-five years ago," I tell him.

"That's even longer than our relationship," Zach says.

Our relationship? What the hell is he talking about? Zach is drinking too much and too fast. So am I for that matter, but at least I had a big lunch and have food in my stomach to help sop up some of the alcohol. I think back to the luncheon and don't remember seeing Zach eat anything. We need to nip the drinking in the bud. I wonder if it's too late to order dinner.

"I'm embarrassed beyond words, and I'd like to amend my earlier suggestion for pretending we both coincidentally walked in here and decided to have a drink together. Instead, I'd like to make believe that tonight didn't happen at all." Zach hangs his head and says, "I'm usually much more cautious, Kaity. I hope you'll forgive me."

The jazz band chooses that moment to take a break, and I excuse myself to go to the Ladies' Room. I pull my cellphone from my purse and call Matt. "Hey," I say when he answers. "Is there any chance, *any chance at all*, you can stop by tonight?"

"I just got out of a meeting and another one is starting in a few minutes," he says, "so tonight isn't good for me."

"It's important, Matt. It doesn't matter how late it would be when you got here, but I really need you tonight."

"Unfortunately, tonight won't work for me."

"When will it work for you?" I ask.

"Probably not until I get back from Arkansas. As I believe I told you, sometime in early December."

Something is very wrong. "We haven't been together in weeks, Matt. I have to travel to Boston next week, and I'll be gone until almost Christmas. Please don't make me beg."

"I'm sorry, Kaity, but I have meetings tomorrow that I still have to prepare—"

I close my phone and drop it back into my purse. So much for having sonar waves as far as Matt is concerned.

I return to the table where my fresh Zinfandel is waiting, along with Zach. Screw ordering dinner and eating, but I'm down for drinking and making merry. I pick up my wine glass and drain it.

Chapter Twenty-Nine

The band members are back from their break, and once again the lounge is filled with the smooth sound of good jazz. I look at my empty wine glass and wish I had another.

Zach looks at his watch. "It's after nine o'clock. Where has the time gone?"

Time flies when you're having fun. Didn't Zach know that? But he looks sort of sad, almost defeated, so he probably isn't having fun.

"I should probably get you home," he says.

There's no way in the world he's in any shape to drive. Nonetheless, I say, "How about one for the road?"

"Really? I thought you'd be tired of listening to me prattle on and on by now."

Remembering the deal I just made with myself to screw eating, but to drink and make merry, I smile a merry smile and say, "I'm enjoying our time together. Let's have another drink."

Zach signals the waiter. "So, tell me about your relationship, Kaity. I hope he's a good guy. You deserve to be happy."

Happy? I'm feeling more like a Sappy.

The waiter returns with our fresh drinks, and Zach toasts the waiter.

Zach is wasted, and it's time to get him out of here. "Let's drink up and hit the road, Zach."

He sings quietly. "Hit the road, Zach, and don't you come back no more— Come on, Kaity, sing with me."

"I didn't mean that literally, Zach. Forgive me for saying so, but I don't think you're in decent enough shape to drive."

He sips his drink. "Would you like to drive?"

"I'm in no shape to drive either." I sip my wine. "Let's just enjoy the music while we finish our drinks."

Zach looks at me with glazed eyes. "You're so lovely, Kaity."

He touches the sleeve of my sweater dress and works the material between his fingers. For the first time, I notice that Zach has large hands and long fingers. Longer fingers even than Matt has, which probably means he also has a—*don't even go there, Kaity*, I scold myself.

He takes back his hand and says, "Your dress is so soft, soft in the way I imagine you are." He sips more of his drink. "Do you remember when we went to Boston a couple months ago?"

"Of course I do," I say, "We won a big case without even going to verdict."

"We did. And you did that victory dance at our celebration party. I wanted to take you into my arms and dance with you. You probably didn't have any idea I wanted to sleep with you."

Holey Moley Fuck! I didn't have a clue. All this stuff he's telling me is new to me.

"And soon, we'll be heading back to Boston again." Zach sighs. He sips his drink again and looks around the cozy lounge. "This place is quite romantic, so it's a good thing we agreed to make believe tonight didn't happen. We did agree, didn't we?"

I look around and agree that the lounge is indeed romantic—and cozy too—and I realize I'm also feeling cozy and romantic. Is it the wine? Probably. But it might be Zach. The longer he talks, the more I like him. Well, I've always liked him, but now I like, like him. Or maybe it's realizing my relationship with Matt has changed, might be coming to an end, and I'm lonely for new love. I sip my wine and say, "I agree that this place is romantic. And the jazz is nice and mellow." And Zach smells really, really good. "Are you wearing Vuitton?" I ask him.

"Yes. It's called Imagination. Do you like it?"

"It's very nice," I say and inhale. "Italian citrus and ginger and something more—cedar, I think. Very pleasant."

He leans toward me and whispers, "I'm using my imagination right now, and I'm imagining what I'd like to do to you." Zach looks into my eyes, his hazel eyes completely glazed over.

Holey Fucking Moley! He's making me fucking wet. "And what's your imagination imagining?" I ask.

"Do I dare tell you, Kaity? It could get me into trouble."

"Since we're pretending tonight didn't happen, what the hell, Zach, go for it."

Zach sighs and touches the sleeve of my sweater dress again. "I'm imagining undressing you, Kaity, pulling your lovely soft dress up and over your head and touching you. Every part of you. Shall I go on?"

I'm sopping. "Please. Go ahead. Tell me more."

"I'm imagining what it would be like to have you naked in my arms, to touch your breasts, to put my fingers inside you. And to make love to you."

Waves of wet are rushing through me—I can almost hear the sound of the white caps breaking in my ears! —and drenching me between my legs.

"Kaity, if you were to touch me, you would have no doubt about how much I desire you."

Touch him? I want to fuck him. But there is no way in hell I can tell him that. I need a cold shower. We need to take a time out. I look at him and sigh. I say, "Maybe we'd better stop here, Zach, and go back to pretending tonight didn't happen before we both get into trouble."

He raises his glass to me and says, "To agreeing to pretend tonight didn't happen, right?"

We touch glasses. "Right," I agree.

"Okay, now we're getting somewhere. So, if we're not driving you home, what are we going to do?"

The Langdon Hotel is located in the AMA building, right across the street in the same building in which the law firm is located. "Maybe we should stay across the street," I suggest.

"At the office?"

He's more wasted than I thought. "No, Zach. Not the office. The Langdon."

He chugs his drink and signals the waiter to bring the check. "Separate rooms?"

Separate rooms will be the only way to avert a disaster. "Yes. Separate rooms."

I finish my wine while we wait for the waiter to return with Zach's credit card. We retrieve our coats from the coatroom and are out the door and on our way to the hotel across the street.

Chapter Thirty

Zach and I cross State Street. Because it's late, the State Street entrance to the AMA building is closed, so we walk around the building to the Wabash Avenue entrance. We enter the hotel lobby, and Zach checks us in. We get into a waiting elevator, and Zach presses the button for our floor. The elevator doors open, and we walk down the corridor to my room. Zach opens the door and hands me my keycard. "I'm right next door, Kaity, so knock if you need anything."

"I had fun tonight, Zach," and I stand on the tips of my toes and kiss him on the cheek. "Are you okay?"

He nods and says, "Sleep well, Kaitlyn." And he continues down the corridor to his room.

~ * ~

I close the door behind Zach and sigh. I hang up my parka in the closet and take my cellphone from my purse. There's no message from Matt, neither voicemail nor email, not even a text. But I feel bad I hung up on him earlier, so I email him:

Hi Matt, I miss you and need to see you. Please make time
for us to be together, even if it's for only an hour or two.
Sending love, Kaity.

I slip my sweater dress over my head and hang it in the closet alongside my parka. I sit down on the bed and slip off my shoes. Wearing only my bra and panties, I pad into the bathroom. There are toothbrushes and toothpaste on the vanity top, and I brush my teeth. I unclasp my bra and hang a strap over the doorknob. I remove my panties and use one of the mini bars of soap the hotel provides to wash them, and I hang them over the shower bar to dry overnight.

I twist my hair up into a knot and pin the knot to the top of my head. I look in the mirror and touch my breasts, wishing Matt was here to touch me. And then I think of Zach and his coppery curls and hazel eyes. And I remember his large hands and long fingers and realize I am squeezing my nipples. Enough!

I turn off the bathroom light and crawl under the blankets, grateful we dodged a bullet.

But I go to sleep thinking about a man who isn't Matt, a tall and slender man with a square jaw. A man who smells like citrus and ginger, who has large hands and long fingers. A man who just spent the last hour imagining making love to me.

~ * ~

I feel him climb into bed behind me, and I inhale his scent. He puts his arms around me and holds me to him. He kisses the back of my neck, and I'm glad I put my hair up. His kisses trail down my neck to my shoulder, and I feel his erection pressing hard against my ass.

I turn toward him, and he kisses me, long and deep, and his lips are on fire. I feel the wet gathering between my thighs, and his large hand goes to my breast. He lowers his hot lips to my nipple and sucks gently, while his fingertips knead my other breast. His tongue goes into my mouth and mates with my own. He inserts a long finger into me and plunges it deep. He adds a second long finger, and his fingers dance inside me. He removes his fingers and moves above me.

He plunges into me, and the wet flows as he thrusts within me. He turns on his side and thrusts again. His large hands are on my ass, pulling me toward him, bringing me closer and closer to him, and he goes deeper into me. He thrusts, and I thrust with him. He pumps, and I pump with him. He pounds, and I pound with him.

I am drenched in wet, dripping, and the waves that wash over me are rogue waves, extreme and unpredictable, and I shudder again as I climax over and over again.

He turns me over, and I rise to my knees when he kneels behind me. He enters me from behind and his large hands hold my breasts, his long fingers kneading and caressing, as he pumps and pounds into me. And the wet gushes from me.

He turns me onto my back and takes my hand. He places it on his erection and covers my hand with his own. And we begin to stroke, my hand moving beneath his, and we stroke until he is enormous.

He moves above me and lifts my legs onto his shoulders. He plunges deep within me, and he thrusts and pounds. I thrust and pound with him, and wave after wave of orgasm surge through my body. I cry out and reach to hold him.

But he's gone.

~ * ~

I sit up in bed. I'm alone and uncovered, the blankets tangled at my feet, and I hold a pillow in my arms. I tremble as I realize I was dreaming of a man with copper-colored hair and hazel eyes. The sheet is damp with my climax, and I shiver. I pull the blankets up and lie back down, wrapping the blankets around me. It takes a long time for me to fall back to sleep.

Chapter Thirty-One

I awaken early and remember my dream. Wow and Holey Moley and Whoa Nellie. Scratch Whoa Nellie. Whoa Nellie is Matt, and I dreamed of Zach.

I get out of bed and check my cellphone. There's a reply from Matt to the email I sent him last night:

> *Hi Kaity, As I've already told you, I probably won't be able to make time for us to get together until early December, but then I may be off again. I'm waiting to hear from my cohorts.*

Great. Just great. And I close my phone.

I shower and dress in yesterday's clothing. Since my panties are still a bit damp, I wrap them in a disposable shower cap and put them in my purse.

I can't stop thinking about my dream. But I also can't help wondering about the change in Matt, and I text him:

> *How's your day going?*

Matt texts back immediately:

> *Ugh. I'll call you later.*

It sounds like his typical day. I drop my cellphone into my purse and think about calling Zach when there's a knock on the door.

It's Zach. As he walks into the room, I remember my dream. I can hardly look at him and feel my face turning red.

"Hi, Kaity, would you like to have breakfast?"

"I probably should head home," I tell him, "but I have to go to the office first and pick up my briefcase."

"I should do that too." Zach leaves a gratuity on a credenza, and says, "I'll get my coat."

I put on my parka while I wait for Zach. He returns a moment later, and we ride the elevator down to the hotel lobby. Zach pushes open the door that leads to the AMA building lobby, and we can see through the floor-to-ceiling windows that it's a sunny November morning. Our shoes tap on the tiled floor as we walk to the northern elevator bank that will take us to our offices on the thirtieth floor.

In the elevator on our way up to the office, Zach says, "I'd like to apologize for my asinine behavior last night."

After the dream I had last night, *I* should be the one to apologize. "No apology necessary," I say. "It was nice to get to know you better." And did I ever.

"After I get my briefcase, I'll bring my car around and pick you up out front on the Wabash side."

"You don't have to drive me home, Zach. You live north and I live west. I can grab an Uber to drop me off at Union Station, and I'll take a Metra train."

"I don't mind driving you, Kaity. It'll give us a chance to talk some more. I might not even embarrass myself,"—he made that sort of half laugh he was doing last night and continues— "since I'm now completely sober in the light of a new day."

"Zach, you did not embarrass yourself," I assure him. After the dream I had, *I'm* the one who should be embarrassed. Thank goodness he doesn't know about my dream. "We're friends and we had a friendly conversation."

"I appreciate that, Kaity. If I'm not driving you home, the least I can do is drop you off at Union Station."

The elevator stops at the thirtieth floor. The doors open, and we exit the elevator. Zach looks at me and says, "I'll get my car and meet you out front." We head in opposite directions up and down the corridor to retrieve our briefcases from our respective offices.

~ * ~

Zach is leaning against his Porsche when I exit the building. The car is a sleek black 911, and he opens the passenger door for me. "Beautiful automobile," I tell him as I get into his car.

"It is a nice ride, that's for sure," he says and closes the door. He walks around the back of the car and gets into the driver's seat. "Union Station? You're sure?"

I nod, and Zach pulls away from the curb. Early on a Saturday morning the downtown traffic is light, and it takes less than ten minutes to arrive at the Adams Street entrance to Union Station.

He gets out of the car and comes around to open the door for me. I stand on the tips of my toes and kiss him on the cheek the way I did last night. But I'm almost waiting for him to put his arms around me and hold me close. "Thanks, Zach. See you at the airport next week."

He gives me a little salute, gets back into his car and drives away.

~ * ~

Because Metra is operating its trains on its Saturday schedule, I have to wait more than an hour for the next train that will bring me home. I go to Starbucks and order an Irish Creme Cold Brew— 'Tis the season—and sit down. While I enjoy my Cold Brew, I check my cellphone again and see an email from Matt:

I have another crisis on my hands, and I'm on my way to
Peoria to deal with it.

96

I slam shut my phone and sip my Cold Brew. Then I open my phone again and begin typing a text to Zach to thank him for—for what? —last night? How should I phrase my text without giving him the wrong idea? I need to think about it and close my phone. I think again about my dream. Wow. I tell myself to forget about the dream and concentrate on how to make things right with Matt.

I decide instead to people-watch as I finish my Cold Brew and wait until it's time to board the train that will take me home.

Chapter Thirty-Two

I arrive home and shrug out of my parka. I hang it in the hall closet and bring my briefcase into my home office. I go into my bedroom and look at myself in the mirror above my dresser. I run my hands down the front of my sweater dress. Zach is right. It is soft, and I touch my breasts. I remove my dress and bra and cover my boobs with my hands, wishing Zach—no, not Zach! *Matt!* —was there to touch me and suck my nipples. It's my dream that's messing with my thinking, but I feel a knot of confusion lodge in my heart.

I fold my dress and place it in my "To the Cleaners" basket. I take my panties from my purse and throw the disposable shower cap into the wastebasket. I toss my panties, along with my bra, into my laundry basket, and touch myself. I am wet, and I insert a finger inside, again wishing—I am surprised to discover I'm not sure who I'm wishing for. The dream again. I change into my running clothes and tie the laces of my sneakers. I put my cellphone in my pocket and go for my usual mile run.

I determine to put Zach out of my mind and think about Matt as I run. I wonder what happened to make Matt want to take a step back from our relationship. Because he has. Regardless of what he's told me, something *has* changed. I don't want to admit it, but things between us lately feel much different than they did before. A lot different.

Has his relationship with his Traveling Partner become intimate again? Would he tell me if it did? What would he say? "FYI, I'm fucking my Traveling Partner again." Since he initially hesitated to tell me that his "sort of" relationship with his Traveling Partner had ended, how the fuck was he going to tell me if it resumed?

Running usually clears my head, and I'm afraid I'm now thinking more clearly than I want to think. And I might have to face up to some things I'm not ready to face. Things I don't want to face at all.

~ * ~

My home phone is ringing when I walk in the door after my run. "Hello."

"Hi Kaity, it's Zach."

Zach, not Matt.

"Are you okay? You sound sort of breathless."

"I just came in from my run, Zach. I'll catch my breath in a minute. So, what's up?"

"I wanted to be certain you got home okay."

"Yes, got home, went for my run, and I'll start my new assignment after a quick shower."

"Take a day off, Kaity. You've got a week to get that report to me, and I have no doubt you will do your usual fastidious work."

"Thanks, Zach, but I have nothing else to do today, so it's a good time for me to get started."

There's a pause.

"Zach?"

"Sorry." He clears his throat. "Since you're not busy, would you like to have dinner with me tonight?"

Maybe I *would* like to have dinner with Zach. At the very least, it will take my mind off Matt and help to keep me from wondering about whether he's resumed his intimate relationship with his TP, which is the way I'm going to refer to his Traveling Partner from now on. "Yes, I would. Thanks for the invite, Zach."

"Is there somewhere special you'd like to go?" he asks.

"I'll be fine with wherever you choose."

"How about Morton's?" he suggests.

"Perfect."

"I'll pick you up at seven o'clock," Zach says and ends the call.

Chapter Thirty-Three

I check my email throughout the afternoon, but there's nothing from Matt since he emailed this morning when he was on his way to Peoria to intercede in another crisis.

The doorbell rings, and I check myself one last time in the bathroom mirror. I'm wearing beltless black slacks and an emerald green long-sleeved silk blouse. I moussed my hair and scrunched it. My fancy gold hoops are in my earlobes, and I applied a bit of light makeup. A spritz of Opium, and I'm ready to greet Zach.

I open the door, and he walks into my living room. "Hey, Kaity, you look great," he says. He laughs and opens his jacket. He's wearing a sweater that's very nearly the same shade of green as my blouse, and his slacks are black.

We're dressed like twins. I laugh with him. "You also look great." And he was great in my dream. Really great. Beyond great. *Stop!* I tell myself.

"Perhaps our clothing choices can be attributed to like-thinking minds," he says. "Ready?"

"I just have to grab my jacket." I take my jacket—a brown suede bomber jacket nearly identical in color to the leather bomber jacket Zach is wearing—from the hallway closet.

He takes my jacket and holds it so that I can put my arms into the sleeves. "Unbelievable," he says, and we laugh together.

~ * ~

100

Zach and I make small talk on the way to Morton's and while we go through the ritual of parking and walking into the restaurant. "Reservation for Eberle," Zach says, and we are seated immediately at a small table in a cozy corner of the restaurant.

He helps me remove my jacket and hangs it over my chairback and does the same with his own. A waiter appears and drops off menus and takes drink orders. Zach looks at me and says, "Presumably we're having steak, so something red?"

I nod, and Zach asks the waiter, "What's your best red?"

"We have a very nice Merlot, sir," the waiter answers.

"Two of the Merlot then, please."

We look over our menus. Hell, we're at Morton's Steakhouse, so of course our choices are rare steaks—a petite filet mignon for me and a New York Strip for Zach. We both order grilled asparagus and start with an order to share of prosciutto wrapped mozzarella.

Our wine arrives, and we touch glasses. "To another nice evening," I propose.

Zach hesitates. "Kaity, again, I want to apologize for my inexcusable behavior last night."

"You've apologized, Zach. And I thought we were pretending last night didn't happen." Last night included my dream, which means it didn't happen either.

"I'll drink to that," he says, and we both sip our wine.

The appetizer arrives, and we fill our plates.

Zach says, "Tell me about your boyfriend. What's his name?"

I chug my wine. "His name is Matt, but he's not really my boyfriend."

"What do you mean?"

Zach is eating and I'm drinking. "I'll try to explain, but I might need another glass of wine to do so."

He signals for the waiter and points at me.

"Aren't you going to have another?"

"After last night, I may never drink again. Except for an occasional glass of wine so that I can properly toast you." He raises his glass, and I do the same.

I finish my wine and set the glass aside. My fresh Merlot arrives with our dinners, and we dig in.

The waiter returns to ask if our meals are satisfactory. Seeing my mostly untouched meal, he asks, "Was there something wrong with your dinner?"

"It was fine," I assure him. "I guess I wasn't as hungry as I thought I was."

He asks if we'd like to see dessert menus. When we both decline, he signals for a busboy.

After our table is cleared, Zach says, "You were about to tell me about Matt, who isn't really your boyfriend."

I sip my wine and say, "Matt and I met a long time ago. We worked after-school jobs at the same grocery store. We became friends, but lost contact after high school when we both started full-time jobs elsewhere."

"That's when you came to the law firm. I remember you were already working at the firm when I came on as a new associate right out of law school."

We talked about that before. "Yes, that's right," I say and sip more of my wine.

"I can't help remembering your Kaitlyn Kinney name plate."

I wonder again why he's so fixated on my name plate. "Matt contacted me a few months ago, in July, and we've been talking, texting, emailing nearly every day ever since. And we've gotten together a bunch of times."

"That sounds like a boyfriend."

"It's complicated though." I sip my wine again and sigh deeply. "We were building a relationship. At least I thought we were. Maybe we are. But I don't know anymore." I finish my wine. "And he was teaching me that naughty could be nice," I say and giggle.

"Whoa," Zach says and puts up a hand. "Stop right there, Kaity. I don't believe I want to hear this."

"Sorry. I'm not a prude, Zach, but Matt was teaching me how to spice things up."

"Kaity, please do not share the details of your private life with me. Not only is it none of my business, but I don't want to know the details."

How can I talk to him about this if I can't give him the details? Perhaps another glass of wine will help. "Could I have another glass of wine, please?"

Zach signals for the waiter and again points to me.

Maybe I can give it a try without giving details. "Is it okay if I talk to you about it, if I leave out personal details?"

Zach nods.

"A few weeks after Matt contacted me, he told me he travels with his TP."

"His tepee?" Zach frowns. "He travels with a tent?"

"Not a wigwam tepee!" I say and giggle again. "His Traveling Partner! TP is what I call her. Matt told me that he and this woman had been Traveling Partners—that's what they call themselves—and that they traveled together in his RV. He told me they were in what he called a 'sort of' relationship for about a year. He said their relationship became intimate, but he ended the relationship a month before he contacted me."

My fresh glass of Merlot arrives, and I sip it. "At first, Matt was calling, emailing or texting me, sometimes ten times a day. But lately, his calls and texts and emails have stopped coming as often. At first, I chalked it up to how busy he is because he's always very busy."

I take another sip of wine. My head spins for a second or two, and I put down my wine glass. "Besides running an insurance business, he is very active in his community, and he ran for office in his township. He gets hundreds of emails and phone calls every day from people wanting him to help them get their utility bills lowered or get a neighbor to lower loud music or listen to their complaints about barking dogs. It's unending. He's also very involved with his Homeowners Association, and the HOA also keeps him busy."

"Matt sounds like a busy guy."

"He is, but he's been busy since he first contacted me. And despite how busy he was, he always found time to call, email or text me, but now there are days when he doesn't email at all. Or call. Or text."

I pick up my glass again and take another sip of my wine. "So, I asked him where I stood in his life. He told me I'm important to him, but he reminded me he had a lot on his plate. He also said he wanted me to realize that even though he ended his relationship with his TP—he called her his Traveling Partner, not his TP—he's still in a relationship with her because they own property together."

"Owning property together would certainly complicate things."

The wine is going down very smoothly, and I sip again. "I asked him if he'd become intimate with his TP again—I didn't say TP to Matt though." I hiccup. "I said Traveling Partner."

Zach rolls his eyes.

"Did you just roll your eyes at me?"

"I might have an eyelash in my eye," Zach says and blinks twice, and I am reminded he has those long thick beautiful lashes.

"Matt said he has no time to even think about intimacy, and that his TP—excuse me, his *Traveling Partner*—hasn't been breaking down any doors to be intimate either."

I take a long swallow of my wine. Whoa. My head spins again as I drain my glass. "Matt also reminded me that the relationship we're building would seem unconventional to many people, and he cautioned me not to be swayed by other people's conventional logic. He said we had a relationship that went back decades, and some people wouldn't understand that. But if we're okay with the way our relationship is developing, it's nobody else's business, and that should be all that matters."

My fingers push my empty wine glass around in circles. "What do you think, Zach?"

"I'm sorry, Kaity, but I'm too biased to give you an honest opinion."

I hiccup again and set aside my wine glass. "Could you at least try?"

"If I tell you this sounds fucked up and Matt is giving you a bunch of bullshit, it might very well be my selfish way of thinking because I have feelings for you myself. I've already admitted I'm in like with you."

"Or in lust," I remind him.

"Or in lust," Zach repeats. "But mostly in like. On the other hand, if I tell you that Matt sounds like an honest guy and you should continue your relationship, then I might be giving you bad advice. I might be telling you what I believe you want to hear because I care about you and want you to be happy."

"But you're such a smart guy, Zach. You're a litigator. You have the ability to see both sides of an issue. I'd like your expert opinion."

He laughs. "I'm no expert on this subject, Kaity. Believe me. Definitely not an expert."

Should I tell him about my dream? "Would it be okay if I tell you about something that happened last night?"

"Of course."

"It's sort of private," I say.

Zach puts his elbows up on the table and holds his head in his hands. "Then I'd prefer that you don't tell me."

I hiccup again. "But it concerns you, Zach, and I think I should tell you."

Zach rolls his eyes again and sighs.

"*That* was an eyeroll."

"Sorry, Kaity," he says and sips his wine. "All right. Tell me."

"I dreamed of you last night, and it was an incredible dream."

"Incredibly good or incredibly bad?"

I take a deep breath before I reply. "I dreamed you made love to me."

Zach looks away, and it looks almost as if he's trying to suppress a smile.

"So that's incredibly good, right?"

Still looking away, he tries to suppress another smile, and then looks back at me.

"I must have used those sonar waves you told me about and pinged you," I say and make a whistling sound, "because your heat-seeking torpedo scored a direct hit."

Zach throws his head back and laughs long and hard.

I guess my whistling sound made him laugh so I whistle again. I wait until his laughter subsides and then add, "We didn't talk, though. Not at all. Not a word, naughty or otherwise."

Zach merely stares at me, wordlessly. Then he points to my empty wine glass and finally speaks. "Would you like another glass of wine, Kaity, or are you ready to go home?"

"Maybe yes and maybe no. Or maybe no and maybe yes. Can you help me out, Zach? What should I do?"

"I probably should take you home."

My head is still spinning, my thoughts are scrambled, and my brain is fried, which probably makes me an egghead. I laugh but don't know why. It's a question I'll have to ponder. "You're right, Zach. I've embarrassed myself enough for one night. Please take me home."

Zach finishes his wine. He pays the check and then drives me home.

Chapter Thirty-Four

I awaken the next morning with a hangover, and my headache gets worse when I remember my obnoxious behavior the night before. Why did I go on and on, telling Zach all that stuff about me and Matt? I can hardly recall the end of the evening, except for a vague recollection of Zach driving me home and escorting me inside. He helped me shrug out of my jacket and hung it in the hall closet. He kissed the top of my head before he shut the door and went on his way.

One thing for sure—Zach and I evened up the score. I swallow a couple of ibuprofens and check my cellphone for voicemail and email. Nothing from Matt. Not even a simple text. I call him, but the call goes straight to voicemail:

Hi Matt, I miss you and hope you're having a good day.

I put my cellphone on the charger and head back to bed.

~ * ~

I'm awakened a few hours later by the ringing of my bedroom telephone. "Hello."

"Hey, Kaity, what's happening?" It's Matt.

Nothing more than my world falling apart, getting wasted with my boss and dealing with a terrible hangover. "Not much," I fib, not wanting to admit how rotten I feel. "I miss you." And because I can't take "no" for an answer, I ask, "Is there any chance of you stopping by?"

"Not today. This week is going to be even busier than usual as I contend with the usual crap and try to wrap things up before I head to Arkansas. I have to help a friend get a tarp over his boat this afternoon, and I have to attend my HOA meeting tonight."

"Will we be able to get together before you go spelunking and treasure hunting?"

"It's unlikely because I have meetings in Springfield on Monday and Tuesday, and I believe we're leaving for Arkansas on Wednesday."

Which means he'll be too busy to spend any time with me. "Same old, same old," I say.

"The very same. Talk to you later," he says and hangs up.

And he wants me to believe that nothing has changed? Does he even remember that I'm leaving for Boston next week and will likely be there through at least the middle of December?

The phone rings again. Maybe he does remember. "Hey."

But it's not Matt. It's Abby Dixon, Zach's assistant.

"Hi Kaity, it's Abby. Zach asked me to call and let you know that the team won't be going to Boston until the Monday after Thanksgiving. There are a couple of team members traveling for Thanksgiving, so Zach didn't want them to have to be concerned about ending their holiday weekend early."

So, Zach had Abby call me instead of calling me himself. That's what I get for making a fool of myself last night. "Thanks, Abby. Are you and Zach working today?"

"Just for a couple of hours. Zach told me he might have a date tonight."

I feel my heart sink. First Matt and now Zach. What did I expect? Zach told me he dates lots of women, and who can blame him? He's such a hunk.

"Has he called yet?" Abby asks.

"Has who called?"

Abby laughs. "Zach! He told me you'd gone out together the last couple of nights, and he was going to call and ask you out again tonight."

My heart begins its climb out of the depths from which it had sunk.

"That's why I'm calling you, rather than Zach calling himself. I guess he didn't want to mix business and pleasure."

"No, he hasn't called yet. Thanks for the heads up."

"I shouldn't be telling you this, but he's been talking about you for quite some time. Wondering about you, asking me questions. But lately, he's talked about you nearly every day. Did I think you were beautiful? Were you dating anyone? That's why I asked you the other day if you were seeing anyone. When you told me you thought the guy was backing off and your relationship was ending, I passed that on to Zach. I hope that was okay, Kaity. Then he wanted to know did I think you'd go out with him."

I sigh, and Abby continues, "He's been trying to work up the nerve to call you for months. I was so glad for him when he told me he'd finally had the courage to ask you out. Zach is such a smart guy, but lately he's been acting like a teenager with a crush. The man is head-over-heels for you, Kaity. You have no idea how far gone he is. Please don't let Zach know I told you this stuff."

"I won't say a word. Thanks, Abby. Hey, how's your fiancé?"

"He's great. Thanks for asking," Abby says, and we end our call.

I'm conflicted. I thought Matt and I were building a relationship. But it seems that Matt wants to back off. I wonder again if he's involved with his TP again.

As for Zach, I know he likes me, but now I just learned his feelings for me are more than platonic. I feel bad that I didn't nip his wandering imagination in the bud the other night after telling me about all those things he imagined. But he smelled so good. And I was so horny.

And I made it worse last night by telling him about my dream. I actually told him I dreamed he made love to me. And then went on about sonar waves and pinging and his torpedo. What the hell is wrong with me? How will I ever be able to face him again? Maybe it will be for the best to decline his invitation to go out tonight when he calls. Put some space between us.

In the meantime, I need to know where Matt and I are in our relationship. But I have no idea how I will be able to do that. I decide to go for a run to clear my head. I change into my running clothes and take my cellphone off the charger. I stick the phone in my pocket and head out the door.

I can smell the changing season in the late afternoon air as I run. On my good days, the autumn leaves are crisp and golden, boasting nearly all the varying colors of the visible spectrum as they crunch beneath my sneakers. On my bad days—if I notice them at all—the leaves are mostly muddy brown and brittle. Today they are somewhere in between.

I return from my run, and my head is as muddled as it was before I ran. I check my phone for messages, but there's nothing from Matt. I undress and take a shower. I feel better after my shower, but I'm still thinking about Matt and wishing I knew where and how I fit into his life. I realize I've become a pushy broad, but I send him an email anyway:

> *Is there ANY chance AT ALL that we might be able to spend some time together?*

I dress in jeans and pull a Chicago Bears T-shirt over my head. I mousse and scrunch my hair and let it air dry while I continue my research. I'm just beginning to write a report when I receive a response to my email from Matt:

> *Not at this time, but I'll keep you posted.*

Really? And nothing has changed? In addition to feeling like a pushy broad, I also feel like a fool, and its high time for this foolish pushy broad to end this farce of a relationship. I write him an email:

> *It's good to know you'll keep me posted, but I don't know anymore where I fit into your life. We haven't made love in weeks, Matt. Weeks! We haven't spent any time together at*

all. You don't seem to be able to make any time for me, and we can't build a relationship if we don't spend any time together. I'm reading between the lines and thinking that building a relationship together isn't in the cards for you. If all you can offer is friendship, I'll accept that, but let's not pretend otherwise.

~ * ~

The hours tick away as I work, and I'm off to a good start on the work Zach needs from me by Friday, or maybe—due to the change in travel plans—he won't need it until the following week. Regardless of when he needs it, the work has to be done, and I continue working.

It's four-thirty when the phone rings. Feeling bummed about the turn my relationship with Matt has taken, I hope it's Matt calling in response to my email to try to make things right between us again.

"Hi, Kaity, it's Zach."

I sigh softly, disappointed it isn't Matt's voice I'm hearing. "Hi, Zach."

"Would you be up for an early dinner tonight?" he asks.

Maybe dinner with Zach will help to take my mind off Matt. I like Zach, but I'm torn because I don't want to give him the wrong idea.

"Kaity? Are you there?"

What the hell. I'll be friendly but not flirty, and hope Zach won't mention my dream or sonar waves. "As long as you accept my apology for my behavior last night and promise not to let me drink."

Zach laughs. "No apology necessary, but we are now square—Even-Steven."

I remember I had a similar thought earlier. "Touché."

~ * ~

I change from my T-shirt into a rose-colored long-sleeved blouse and tuck it into my jeans. Zach arrives at my home at six-thirty, tall and handsome, dressed in jeans and a white shirt. And his scent is as sensational as it always is.

We have dinner at Riccardo's and talk and laugh while we dine. I'm surprised at how much I enjoy being with him.

He brings me home after dinner and says, "I'm sorry this has to be an early night, Kaity, but I've got so much work to do."

"Don't apologize, Zach. I get it."

"I know you get it, and it makes life so much easier not having to explain."

"Thank you for another nice dinner, Zach. I had fun."

"Me too." He leans down and kisses me on the cheek. "Good night, Kaity. I hope your dreams are sweet and incredibly warm."

Just when I thought I'd gotten away with Zach not making any mention of dreams, he dispels me of the notion, and I feel myself blush. At least he said warm and not heat-seeking.

And Zach leaves me at my door with a smile on his face.

Chapter Thirty-Five

I get downtown early Monday morning and go directly to my office. I'm hard at work researching and writing, and I find a case I think Zach will be able to cite as precedent in the brief he's writing. I scan it, and I'm about to email it to him when the phone rings. Abby Dixon's name comes up in the caller ID screen.

"Hey Abby," I say.

"Hey, Kaity. How are things going between you and Zach?"

"He's a good guy, Abby. We're getting to know each other, and I'm enjoying spending time with him."

"He is terrific, Kaity, and speaking of spending time together, Zach just asked me to reserve a section for the team at Radio Room tonight for Monday Night Football, and I ordered a whole slew of yummy appetizers. And speaking of Zach, he wants to talk to you. One moment."

And then Zach is on the line. "Good morning, Kaity. Have you had any luck finding any cases on point?"

"Yes, several, and I just now found one that's right on the money. I scanned it and I'm about to email it to you. You'll have it shortly."

"Thanks, Kaity. That's my girl."

Was I more flirty than friendly? I must be giving him the wrong idea.

"Can I count you in to join the team to watch the game tonight at Radio Room?"

"Count me in. It sounds like fun."

"We'll meet in the lobby at seven o'clock and walk over."

"See you then." Friendly not flirty, I remind myself. Friendly not flirty.

~ * ~

The team meets in the AMA lobby and heads over to Radio Room. The sports bar is located at the corner of State and Kinzie. We walk en masse across the two streets and arrive as one, and head to the section Zach reserved for us.

Coats and jackets are hung on the backs of chairs, and we load up our plates at the buffet table that's set up with chicken tenders, fried pickles, truffle fries, fried cheese curds, chicken wings, crispy calamari and rock shrimp, all with the proper dipping sauces.

Michael, my paralegal counterpart, sits at a table with the litigation associates—Jason Whitely, Stefanie Jones and Gregory Norris—so I join Abby and her counterpart, Maria Shue, at another table. Zach takes the fourth seat beside me. His scent is intoxicating as it always is, and I inhale its essence.

A server brings a couple of pitchers of beer and four beer mugs to our table. The group chats for a bit, and then Abby and Maria go back to the buffet table for second helpings. Zach has his cellphone out. "Please excuse me, Kaity, but I have to take this call."

He walks away to a quieter part of the room, and I pull out my own cellphone from the pocket of my jeans. I open my phone and see there's an email from Matt. I open the message and read it:

> *Hi Kaity, in response to your email, I still don't know in what direction I'm headed. I don't want to fill you with false hope or mislead you, and I don't want you to place your life on hold. I'm sorry, Kaity. Sending love, Matt.*

I don't want to believe the words my eyes just read. It doesn't seem possible. It can't be. A couple of weeks ago, Matt and I were making love and talking about building our relationship, maybe sharing our lives.

But why am I surprised? I've known in my heart that things had changed, and its long past time for me to put on my big-girl panties and face that I'd been right about Matt wanting to step back, to end our relationship. I feel the tears begin to build behind my eyes, and I will myself not to cry. I look up at the ceiling and squeeze my eyes shut before the tears can fall. I put my cellphone back into my pocket.

Zach returns and apologizes. "Sorry, Kaity. A friend of mine had a crisis brewing earlier today, and asked if I'd keep myself available tonight in case he needed my help with something. His crisis has been resolved, thankfully, so there won't be any more annoying calls to ruin the evening."

I don't respond. Can't respond.

"Kaity? What's the matter? Are you alright?"

"I'm sorry, Zach. Please excuse me for a moment," and I head to the Ladies' Room.

Chapter Thirty-Six

As I enter the Ladies' Room, I nearly collide with a woman who's on her way out, shouting into her cellphone, "It's time for you to wake up and face that the man isn't in love with you!" I am startled. I look back over my shoulder, and the woman mouths an apology. But it isn't the woman's shouting that startles me. It's her words.

I remain stunned and feel a chill in my heart because the woman might as well have been shouting at me. I stand at the wash basin and look into the mirror, and my face is nearly the color of the white blouse I'm wearing. It's as if I've been hit squarely between my eyes and a barrel of cold water poured over my head. A veil suddenly lifts, and curtains part in an instant. It all comes down to one simple fact—Matt is not in love with me.

If I'm honest with myself, deep down in my heart of hearts, on some level I've known it all along. There was never any talk of love. The one and only time I'd dared—yes, dared—to tell Matt I'd fallen in love with him was early in our relationship when he'd been asleep and wouldn't hear me because I'd had a sense, even then, that he didn't want to hear words of love.

In matters of the heart, I have an uncanny ability to see only what I want to see, and anything that doesn't fit within my vision of what I want life to be is ignored, disregarded. I have a tendency to look through rose-colored glasses and hope for the best. It's gotten me into trouble in the past and no doubt contributed to me being a two-time loser. And now it's three strikes. I should have learned my lesson long before now.

Matt probably resumed his relationship with his TP weeks ago and didn't have the courage to tell me. Instead, he backed off, put distance between us, and hoped I'd take the hint. But just as I see only what I want to see, if hints don't meet my perception of what life should be, they fall by the wayside, get trampled on and never see the light of day.

It's strange, but I suddenly feel a sense of freedom, free from having to wonder and worry about my relationship with Matt anymore. It's almost a relief to finally admit to myself that our relationship was all about sex and never about love. I take my phone from my pocket and read again Matt's email. And then I respond:

I hope your internal compass will help you find the direction in which you want to head and lead you to whatever it is you're looking for. I wish you all the best. Kaity.

And that is the end of that.

~ * ~

I go back to the table and sit. Abby and Maria haven't returned, and only Zach remains. I down my beer and pour myself a new one.

"Kaity, is something wrong?"

I don't want to spoil the evening, so I chug my beer and pull myself up by my bootstraps. "Matt emailed me a while ago that he still hasn't decided in what direction he wants his life to go, so I guess our budding relationship has bit the dust."

"You must be disappointed, Kaity, so I'm sorry to hear that."

"Thanks, Zach."

"Are you okay?"

"Yes, or at least I will be."

I finish my beer and stand. "I don't want to be a party pooper, so I'm going to head home."

Zach also stands and says, "I'll drive you."

"Thanks, Zach, but I can Uber."

"I'd like to drive you." He gives his credit card to Abby to settle the tab after the game and grabs our jackets. He takes my arm and says, "Let's go."

We say our good nights and make our way out of the sports bar amid a mix of curious glances and knowing smiles from the team.

~ * ~

The drive home is mostly quiet, Zach seeming to understand my inability to talk yet about the end of my relationship with Matt, and I manage to hold back my tears.

But what am I doing? I should have insisted on Ubering myself home. Zach is too nice a guy to be misled. It's wrong, and I need to set things straight before somebody gets hurt. And I will do that as soon as I'm thinking more clearly.

We make small talk until we arrive at my house. Zach parks in my driveway, and I sigh and say, "I finally realized that my relationship with Matt was not the kind of relationship I'd hoped it would be."

Zach reaches for my hand and holds it. "I'm sorry things didn't work out as you'd hoped, Kaity."

"It's been more than several weeks since Matt and I spent any time together. I suspected that he was backing away, and that our relationship was changing, I kept telling myself that we could fix things, making excuses because I didn't want the relationship to end. But it wasn't that things had changed between us. It's that we each wanted different things. I just didn't want to face it."

"In my opinion, Matt is a foolish guy. Very foolish. Out of his mind foolish. He has no idea what he's giving up."

"You're a sweetheart for saying that" I say and squeeze Zach's hand.

Zach squeezes back and I go on. "This might sound a bit odd, but I've been wondering and worrying about this for weeks, so it's almost a relief it's ended. Does that make sense?"

"It sounds perfectly logical to me."

"I don't have a good track record when it comes to matters of the heart. My first marriage probably ended because we were too young to know what marriage and commitment were all about, and my husband hadn't had a chance to sow his wild oats. The second marriage should never have happened in the first place. I knew almost immediately that I made a mistake and should have ended it long before I did, but I was a fool. Two failed marriages and now this. I thought this third time would be the charm. Instead, I struck out."

"You have a right to feel disheartened, Kaity. When hopes and dreams are shattered, I imagine it's tough to feel any other way."

"Have you heard that old saying, that it's better to have loved and lost than never to have loved at all?"

"I've heard it, of course, but I don't know the answer."

"You told me you've never been in love, Zach. I hope this won't sound insensitive, but you're way the hell better off."

"I hope you're wrong about that, Kaity."

"Take it from me, Zach. Better to have loved and lost is complete and utter bullshit because loving and losing hurts like hell. It brings you down. Way down."

"I'm going to do my best to pick you up again." He puts his fingers beneath my chin and lifts. "Chin up, Kaity. Okay?"

"Thanks, Zach. Again, apologies for spoiling Monday Night Football."

"You didn't spoil anything."

Of course he'd say that. "Thanks for driving me home."

"It was my pleasure," he says, and walks me to my door.

"Would you like to come in and watch the rest of the game?"

"I should go."

I stand on the tips of my toes and kiss him.

Zach kisses me back and says again, "I should go."

And he gets back in his car to make the drive back to the city.

Chapter Thirty-Seven

I awaken refreshed, surprised that I slept as well as I did, and even more surprised that I haven't shed a single tear over Matt. I keep hearing the chorus from Chely Wright's "Shut Up and Drive" in my head and find myself singing it aloud, reminding myself I'll only be missing the man I wanted him to be.

I shower and go for a run and come home feeling invigorated and ready to work. I turn on the computer in my home office, and I'm abstracting a deposition when my phone rings.

"Good morning, Kaity," Zach says. How are you this morning?"

"I'm good. Thanks again for getting me home last night."

"I was happy to do it."

"And thanks for allowing me to whine, Zach. It helped to get that stuff out of my head. So what can I do for you on this bright sunny morning?"

"Nothing this morning, but could I interest you in having dinner with me tonight?"

"Sure. I'll be able to whine with my wine."

He laughs. "I had that thought and almost suggested it, but I'm glad you're the one who said it out loud."

I laugh. "I might have to get you for that."

"I am yours to get."

When I don't immediately respond, he says, "I apologize if that was out of line."

"Heat-seeking torpedo was out of line."

Zach laughs again. "More hilarious than anything."

"In that case, I'm going to raise a glass to your sense of humor. What time tonight?"

"I'll pick you up about six o'clock. Is Wildfire okay?"

"Wildfire's fine," I say. "I'll see you at six."

"See you then."

~ * ~

I work until five and turn off my computer. I shower and dress in beige cargo pants and a grey knit sweater, and I'm ready when Zach arrives at exactly six o'clock. He's wearing navy blue dress slacks and a light blue dress shirt beneath his bomber jacket. He really is a hunk.

"You look terrific, Kaity."

"Thanks, Zach. As do you."

He smiles and holds my jacket, and I slip my arms into the sleeves.

We drive to Wildfire and valet Zach's Porsche.

We check our jackets and sat at a small table. Zach orders a bottle of Cabernet Sauvignon from the wine list. We enjoy our steak dinners and our wine and decline dessert.

We talk about the upcoming trial and Zach says, "I believe we're in good shape."

"For sure your paralegals are. Michael and I have a conference call scheduled for tomorrow. After our call, we'll have all the documents you need FedExed to the office for a morning delivery the following day."

"Perfect. Those materials will come in handy for the work I have to do this weekend," Zach says.

"Michael and I will have finished our assignments by tomorrow afternoon, so let us know if you need our help with anything else."

"Thanks, Kaity. You guys are the best, and I'll keep that in mind."

"Have you noticed I haven't whined?" I ask.

"I did notice. I believe we should have another glass of wine so we can toast to no whining with wine."

Our waiter stops by to refill our wine glasses. "Perfect timing," we say together and laugh.

Zach raises his glass and says, "To wine without whining."

"To wine without whining," I say and lift my glass. "I'll drink to that, but I was planning to whine with my wine."

"Feel free to whine, Kaity, and we'll drink to that as well." We touch glasses and sip our wine.

Facing the fact that my relationship with Matt has ended has given me a whole new sense of freedom, now that I don't have to wonder about it anymore. "I suddenly can't think of anything to whine about," I say and reach for Zach's hand. "Thanks for helping me get through this rough patch, Zach."

He takes my hand and holds it. "I don't know that I helped with anything, Kaity. I'm just glad to see you smiling again."

"You helped more than you know."

We sit quietly, holding hands while we finish our wine.

"Since I'm driving, I'll take a pass, but would you like another glass of wine?"

"Thank you, but I'll also pass. We've got a lot of work to do tomorrow, so you probably should get me home."

"As you wish," Zach says.

He settles our bill, and we retrieve our jackets from the coat check. As always, Zach holds my jacket making it easy for me to slip my arms into the sleeves. We make our way out of the restaurant and wait for the valet to bring Zach's car, and then we head for my house.

Zach walks me to the door and leans down to kiss me, full on the lips this time. His kiss is sweet and gentle with the promise of more, and I kiss him back.

"I should go," he says, just as he said last night.

We kiss again, and then Zach heads back to his car.

Chapter Thirty-Eight

Monday and Tuesday pass in a blink, and already it's Wednesday. The days before Thanksgiving have flown by as members of the trial team are all busy with our assignments—the attorneys writing their briefs and motions, the paralegals shepping cases and checking citations, abstracting depositions, researching case law and preparing case summaries, and the secretaries doing a little bit of everything—before the team heads to Boston next week.

I work in my home office, prepping for my conference call with Michael Cole. As I mentioned to Zach last night, Michael and I scheduled a conference call for this morning.

Our call lasts for more than two hours as Michael and I compare notes and make certain we've put together all the documents that Zach will need. We go down our checklists to be sure we didn't forget anything, and we're both feeling confident that we'll have our assignments completed later today. I tell Michael that I'll call FedEx to schedule late-afternoon pickups at both our homes, and let Abby know that Zach will have our completed assignments tomorrow morning.

I finish my assignment and call FedEx to schedule pickups from both Michael's and my homes. I then call Abby to give her the FedEx tracking numbers for tomorrow's morning delivery.

I check my email, but there's nothing from Matt. Of course there isn't, and I deserve a kick in the ass for being such a fool.

I turn off my computer and printer and end the workday with a shower.

~ * ~

I'm toweled off and in my robe when the phone rings. My heart misses a beat. I remember Zach's kiss last night and hope it's Zach who's calling.

It's Zach, and my heartbeat quickens. "Hi, Kaity. Do you like to dance?"

"I love to dance!" I tell him.

"There's a place not too far from you called Dance! Have you been there?"

"I've never been there, but I like the name of the place, which speaks for itself," I say and laugh.

"They feature bands and DJs, and they alternate sets. Both the bands and the DJs play a lot of Oldies but be forewarned I am an Oldies buff."

I laugh. "Likewise. And I know all the words."

"Then we can sing along together," Zach says and laughs. "How about if I pick you up at seven-thirty?"

"Perfect."

"Wear your dancing shoes," Zach advises. "I'll see you in an hour."

I can hear the smile in Zach's voice and feel a smile of my own painting my face.

Way to go, Kaity. So much for setting Zach straight. But I haven't gone dancing in ages. And maybe there won't be any need to set Zach straight after all.

~ * ~

I look through my closet and choose a black pleated skirt and a black knit top with a three-quarter sleeve. I put up my hair and insert small gold hoops into my earlobes. I line my eyes to highlight their deep green color, and I'm happy with my appearance. What shoes should I wear? I decide on a comfortable pair of flats. Perfect for dancing.

I hope Zach won't be suited up like Johnny Cash tonight. Dressing like twins again would be—what? —embarrassing? coincidental? Does it matter? He won't be wearing a skirt, so there's that.

I put my ID, some cash and my cellphone into a small clutch bag and clip it to the waistband of my skirt, and I'm ready when Zach arrives.

He's wearing pleated black trousers—pleated like my skirt! —and a leather belt with a silver buckle. His shirt is a long-sleeved indigo blue, which makes a nice contrast to his coppery hair. He's unbelievably handsome. Truly an incredible hunk.

I stand on tiptoe to kiss his cheek, and it's a stretch. Did he grow taller overnight, or have I shrunk? My shoes. I need to change my flats and wear shoes with at least a bit of a heel. "I think I need to change my shoes, so I'll be able to reach you. How tall are you?"

"About six-four. Don't change your shoes, Kaity. If you have trouble reaching me, I'll sweep you off your feet."

He might already have done that. I smile up at him and inhale his scent. He holds my coat while I slip my arms into the sleeves, and we are out the door and on our way to dance the night away.

Chapter Thirty-Nine

Zach and I arrive at Dance! and check our coats. We sit side by side at a small corner table, and a moment later a server arrives to take our drink orders.

Zach looks at me, and I say, "I'll have a Zinfandel."

"Scotch for me," Zach says.

"Neat or over ice?" the server asks.

"Neat, and please bring us water," Zach says, and the server hurries away to get our drinks.

The band is on stage and begins playing a medley of Oldies. "Care to dance?" Zach asks.

He takes my hand, and we walk out to the dance floor. We dance and sing along with the Four Tops to "If I was a Carpenter," with the Moody Blues to "In Your Wildest Dreams," and with Randy and the Rainbows to "Denise." Zach is an excellent dancer, and he twirls me and spins me and dips me, and I follow his lead.

We return to our table and sit, chugging our water before sipping our drinks.

"That was so much fun, Zach."

"More fun than I've had in a long time."

The DJ comes on stage and "The Lion Sleeps Tonight" by The Tokens begins to play.

"This place is great. How did you find this place?"

"Believe it or not, Kaity, I am more than a litigator," he says and laughs. "I actually have a life."

"Of course you do. So, tell me about your life. The more-than-a-litigator part of your life."

"I'm an only child, born in Chicago. My folks still live here. I've traveled extensively, and I've met some wonderful people. I have a lot of friends, but nobody too close. I tend to keep to myself. Tell me about you."

"I'm also an only child, also from Chicago, and my folks also still live here."

We fist bump, and I continue. "I also have a lot of friends, but I don't have any best friends. I wonder if that comes from being an only child, where we get used to having to navigate life on our own."

"I haven't thought about it that way, but you may be on to something."

"Maybe," I say, "but that's where our similarities end. The only traveling I've done was going to San Francisco." I finish my drink. "It was the mistake of a lifetime."

"Do you want to tell me about it?"

I groan softly. "Maybe some other time. Let's just have fun tonight."

"As long as you know I'm here for you," he says and finishes his drink.

The server stops by, and we order another round of drinks. "Another Zinfandel for the lady," Zach tells the server, "but please make mine a Scotch on the rocks this time."

We listen to Cream's "White Room" and tap our feet, sort of bopping along with the music. The DJ announces that next up is "Needles and Pins" by the Searchers. Zach stands and extends his hand to me. I take his hand and he leads me back onto the dance floor. We dance and sing along with the Searchers and continue dancing to Gloria Estefan's energetic "Everlasting Love," after which we go back to our table and gulp water. The next song is Peter and Gordon's "World Without Love," and we sing along.

The band changes places with the DJ, and their first song is Fleetwood Mac's "Gypsy," and it's followed by Jon Secada's "Just Another Day."

"Could we dance again?" I ask.

"Of course," he says, and leads me back onto the dance floor.

I smile up at Zach. The next song is Simple Minds, "Don't You Forget About Me," and we continue dancing. "Try" by Pink is next, and Zach and I sing along with the band's excellent female vocalist as we dance.

We go back to our table and are grateful that our server has brought a couple more bottles of water. We sit and chug our water.

The DJ is back, and he starts his new set with my all-time favorite, "Unchained Melody." I love this song and want to dance. The Righteous Brothers have just begun singing, and I look at Zach. "May I have this dance?" I ask. I'm feeling especially warm and romantic and almost add the words "for the rest of my life." I'm content when Zach extends his hand to me, and we return to the dance floor. He takes me into his arms and holds me close.

The song ends, and we return to our table. When Gene Chandler's "Duke of Earl" begins to play, we tap our feet and bop our heads along with the music.

The server stops by with another offer of fresh drinks and goes to fetch them. Phil Phillips' version of "Sea of Love" begins to play. I look at Zach, and he takes my hand and leads me back to the dance floor. I breathe him in when he takes me into his arms and holds me close again. We dance to the next song as well, which is Procal Harum's "Whiter Shade of Pale," and then continue dancing to Heart's "Alone."

We go back to our table when the music ends and the DJ exits. Our fresh drinks arrive, and I dip my finger into my fresh Zinfandel and suck my finger. I look around and decide this place is every bit as cozy and romantic as the Tortoise Club lounge was, and I realize that I'm feeling warm and romantic. Is it the wine? Probably. But it might be Zach. Or maybe it's a combination. I sip my wine and say, "Zach, do you remember how cozy and romantic we thought the lounge was the other night?"

Zach takes a long look at me and nods.

"I'm feeling warm and romantic myself," I say.

"Please don't toy with me, Kaity." His hazel eyes are blazing and surrounded by his long dark lashes, his eyes shine like starbursts.

"I would never do that, Zach. Something you should know about me is that honesty is very important to me. I am honest to a fault and if I say something, I mean it."

"Same here," he says and lifts his glass. "Let's drink to that." I touch my glass to his and sip my wine.

The band comes back onto the stage, and "I Confess" is the band's first choice. Zach says, "The New Colony Six is one of Chicago's own, Kaity. We may have an obligation to dance to this one," and he takes my hand and twirls me around the dance floor as he sings into my ear.

We return again to our table, and Zach orders another round of drinks. And then the band announces that they have a special request for "Vesuvio."

"Do you know 'Vesuvio,' Kaity?"

"It's Furio's song from *The Sopranos*," I say.

We stand together as the music begins and join one other couple on the dance floor. Zach and I look deeply into each other's eyes and join hands, dancing side by side, moving our feet. We dance, our eyes locked on one another, as we lift our arms and bend our elbows, our hands and fingers completely enmeshed, our feet continuing to move, keeping time.

Raising our arms above our heads, I stand behind Zach, and I reach up to place my hands on his shoulders, and his hands cover mine, our hands touching and our feet moving, always keeping time. Turning toward one another and smiling, hooking arms, spinning with arms intertwined, our hands high in the air above our heads, our fingers waving, never losing eye contact with each other. And Zach and I continue to dance.

The band has taken a page out of the book of the Italian group Spaccanapoli and are very near as good. The music is seductive and the singers outstanding, and the female vocalist superb. My heart is pounding as loud as the percussionist's sticks are beating his drums and as hard as his hands are pounding his bongos. And the pipes are out of this world amazing! It's as if Zach and I are the only two people in the room, and it's the most sensual dance of my lifetime. It feels more like making love than dancing, and the wet begins to gather between my legs as we dance.

When the music ends, we are the only couple still standing on the dance floor, and people applaud. Zach and I stand there, our eyes still locked on one another. It seems as if we are in a trance. The band plays a riff that takes us out of our stupor, and we return to our table and sit.

Zach embraces me and kisses me long and deep. "I've been wanting to do that for a long time," he tells me, and he kisses me again, long and deep, this time with tongue.

I feel the knot lodged in my heart begin to unravel. "Do you want to come home with me, Zach?"

"Are you ready to go home?"

"Yes, and I'd like you to come home with me."

Zach nods. He settles the bill, and then we go to retrieve our coats and Zach's car.

Chapter Forty

We arrive at my house, and I hang our coats in the hall closet. "Would you like a drink, Zach? I've got Scotch." I point to a tall cabinet in my living room and say, "It's in that cabinet. I'll get you a glass. Would you like ice?"

"Yes, please," he says.

I return to the living room a moment later with a glass filled with ice and a wine glass of Zinfandel. I hand Zach his glass and turn on the CD player in the sound system that my folks gave me once upon a time. "Do you like Bocelli?" I ask.

"He's one of my favorites," Zach says and pours Scotch over the ice.

"Then Bocelli it will be," I say. I pop my Bocelli CD into the CD player and press play.

I sit beside Zach on the sofa, and he touches my glass with his. "I wish I had something clever to say," he says.

"How about, 'here's lookin' at you, kid,'" I suggest.

Zach pretends to groan and sips his Scotch.

We sit back and listen to the soothing sound of Bocelli while we sip our drinks. When *"Con Te Partirò"* plays, I say, "This is such a sad song."

"Translated, '*Con Te Partirò*' means 'Time to Say Goodbye,'" Zach tells me.

"Goodbyes can be heartbreaking," I say, "and this song feels as if it was written to make the listener cry." I look into Zach's eyes and say, "Please don't say goodbye to me, Zach."

"There's not a chance in hell of that happening, Kaity."

I sigh and sip my wine. "Would you like another Scotch? I'll get more ice," I offer.

"Thank you, but no. I'm good."

I look at Zach and say, "I had so much fun tonight. Thank you for a terrific evening."

"I should be thanking you, Kaity," Zach says. "You made the evening terrific for me. The music tonight was perfect for tripping the light fantastic, and it made for a fantastic evening as well."

"And dancing with you to 'Vesuvio' was so sensual, almost seductive."

"It was sensual, intoxicating," Zach agrees, "extremely so."

Zach is turning out to be a man after my own heart. Of course, he told me that, didn't he? I dip a finger into the remnants of my wine and brush Zach's lips with my wine-laden fingertip. "There's only one way for me to taste my wine now," and I lick his lips with my tongue.

Zach sets his glass aside and takes my wine glass from me and sets it aside as well. Then he takes me into his arms and kisses me—a long, deep passionate kiss.

I want to mold myself to him and I do—chest to chest, tummy to tummy and thighs to thighs—and I feel the length of him harden against me. "I want you to make love to me, Zach," I say.

"You've just ended a relationship, Kaity, and may be on the rebound. That's not the best way to begin a relationship. We probably should pretend that tonight didn't happen, just as we did the other night. I would not forgive myself if you later have regrets."

I remember thinking I might have regrets if my previous relationship didn't work out. Regrets? I suppose I have a few. But does that mean I shouldn't chance a relationship with Zach? I don't know, but I'm willing to take a chance to find real love. "I might have regrets if we do, but I'm certain I'll have regrets if we don't."

I remove the pins from my hair and shake my head so that my hair frames my face. I wrap my arms around Zach's neck and look into his eyes. "And there will be nothing to forgive, Zach. I don't want to pretend tonight didn't happen. I want to remember it for the rest of my life."

I want him. I need him. My very existence depends on him making love to me. At least that's what it feels like to me at that moment. I ache for him in a way I've never ached before. Zach is wavering. I can feel his indecision. If I'm in possession of any kind of sonar waves, real or imagined, now is the time to use them. With my eyes still locked on his, I speak a single word. "Ping."

And then his hand is on my leg and up my thigh and under my skirt and between my legs, and wet continues to gather and soak me.

"We might be more comfortable in my bedroom," I say.

Zach takes my hand and says, "Lead the way."

~ * ~

We hold hands as we stand facing one another in my bedroom. Zach's hazel eyes are blazing with those bursts of brown and gold starlight. "You're so beautiful, Kaity," he says and lowers his head to kiss me. I kiss him back and lean into him, molding my body to his.

He lifts my knit top and pulls it up over my head, and then his hands reach behind me to unclasp my bra. He tosses both articles of clothing onto a chair and brings his hands to my breasts and gently caresses them. Feeling Zach's hands on me for the first time makes me even wetter.

I unbutton his shirt. I slip out of my shoes and step out of my skirt and toss everything onto the chair with the rest of my clothing.

Zach lifts me into his arms and lays me down on my bed. I unbuckle his belt and touch his groin. He's rock hard beneath his clothing. I unzip him and see that his Jockeys can hardly contain him. I want to reach in and free his erection. Before I do, Zach removes the rest of his clothing and tosses it all onto the chair with mine. Like his hands and his fingers, his dick is large and long, and very thick. I feel the wet increase as my eyes feast on this beautiful man.

He lays down beside me and kisses me again. His hands and lips are drawn to my breasts, and his fingertips gently knead and massage them, and then he lowers his head, and his tongue circles my nipples. His lips pull at a nipple and sucks it into his mouth, and he sucks softly and deeply and then gives the same attention to my other breast, his fingers hot and his tongue on fire, as he touches and tastes my nipples.

I'm so aroused that I moan aloud. My body is wriggling in pleasure, as his hands and lips continue to explore my body, moving down to my waist and thighs, first tasting, then plunging his tongue into me, causing me to cry out again as a climatic wave rolls over me. His hands reach up to hold my breasts and his fingers touch my nipples again, while his tongue continues to fuck me.

I bend my legs at my knees and open them wide. "I want to feel you inside me, Zach."

He inserts a long finger into my opening and then two long fingers. Seemingly satisfied that I'm ready for him, he looks into my eyes and moves above me, placing the tip of his dick at my opening and rubbing it against me. I gasp in bliss as he slightly penetrates but withdraws again. I'm panting and squirming. His throbbing cock, moist with my wetness, penetrates again, a little deeper this time, and I feel my body stretching to accommodate his massive erection. Again, he pulls out, and my arms pull him to me, digging my fingertips into his back. He lifts my ass, holding my legs to allow his pulsating cock to slide in deeper this time, but not quite all the way.

A moment later, he slides his cock further inside me, deeper and deeper still. Then he plunges into me, and his cock fills me. My inner muscles expand and contract as I squeeze him tight, pulling him into me. He slides back out and comes back slowly, bringing me to a frenzy. I continue to writhe and moan beneath him, having orgasms beyond belief.

He fills me up and we become one, and I am drenched as waves of wet surge through me. Zach thrusts and pounds, in and out, and thrusts and pounds some more. Still looking into my eyes, he kisses me, and his thrusting and pounding continues.

I am close to climax, and I lift my hips, thrusting along with him, and my wet flows over him. I shudder as a new wave washes over me, and

I feel Zach climax with me. He pulls me close and holds me in his arms and his scent becomes part of me.

"Your Ping was priceless," Zach says and kisses me. "And you are more amazing than I imagined you would be."

"I'm going to clean you up."

"I can do that, Kaity."

"I mean I'm going to clean you up with my tongue and with my lips," and I lower my mouth and lick the come still on his cock and suck him for good measure.

"You're going to make me hard again."

"I hope so," I say and suck him into my mouth, and I suck longer and deeper until he's erect again. I suck hard and pull him in, and Zach begins to thrust, faster and faster, and I suck him just as fast. He thrusts up and into my mouth and pumps until his come fills my mouth. He thrusts a final time, and when my mouth is filled with his creaminess, I swallow and lick his cock clean. Then I crawl up to rest my head on his chest.

"That was incredible, Kaity. Even without spicy chatter."

I lift my head and look at him.

He smiles and kisses me. "I'm teasing."

It seems more like a challenge than a tease. Naughty talk likely will add another dimension to our lovemaking, and my wet begins to flow. "I want to fuck you again," I say, and roll onto my back. I bend my legs at my knees and open my legs. I touch myself until I am sopping wet, and he strokes his dick as he watches. Then I insert a finger and moan aloud, never taking my eyes from his. His already-hardening dick is in his hand as he watches me finger fuck myself.

I get up on all fours, and Zach kneels behind me. He rubs his hands up and down my back and then up and down my front, holding my breasts and tweaking my nipples. His hand reaches between my legs and his fingers test my wetness. I am wet and juicy, and his finger plunges deep inside me, making me cry out. "Talk to me, Kaity."

"Put your cock in me, Zach."

He inserts his large and throbbing dick, pushing slowly into me. "Tell me what you want."

"I want you to fuck me."

And he does. His hands on my hips, he plunges into me, withdraws a bit, then thrusts and plunges again. He pumps and pounds, and I pump and pound with him, matching his thrusts, and the wet that gushes from me allows me to accommodate his large cock.

"Get ready for me to fuck you hard and long, Kaity," and he pumps and pounds faster and harder, thrusting and driving with lust and passion, going deep into me, and I respond with my own thrusts.

He withdraws again and says, "I'm going to fuck you until you beg me to stop," and then he lifts his hips and penetrates me again, plunging into me and thrusting and pounding and pounding some more.

I pound with him, his cock deep inside me, and his balls slap against my ass, and a river of wet oozes from me. The thrusting and pounding continues as his cock touches every part of me, reaching places never having been touched before, and I cry out as waves of orgasm rush through me and send my juices flowing over his cock.

He withdraws his cock and turns me onto my back again. He lifts my legs onto his shoulders and plunges his enormous erection into my opening. "You haven't begged me to stop, and I'm going to fuck you until you do."

There's no fucking way that's going to happen. I'm amazed at his stamina, but he'll give up before I give in. "Fuck me harder," I say.

And his next thrust is huge, and he pushes and pounds into me, thrusting again and again, and I continue to push and pound and match his thrusts. I reach new heights with each new thrust, keeping pace with him. And I work my inner muscles to contract and relax, to pull him in and release, pull and let go, and I am wetter than I've ever been, and my wet flows from out of me and onto him.

And when our simultaneous climax finally comes, we are powerless to stop it, our bodies convulsing together and becoming one, as I have a series of strong orgasms at the very same moment that Zach's come is running up his cock, rising to the top, and he releases everything he has into me.

We shudder and shiver together and then tumble onto my bed. We lie beside one another as we catch our breath. I'd never been made love to with that kind of intensity before. I turn to him, then touch my fingertips to his lips and whisper his name. "That was truly incredible."

"As incredible as was your dream?"

"What's the superlative to even better?"

"Best? You are the most sensual and sexual woman I've ever known, Kaity. I may not be certain of the superlative for best, but *that*—what we just did—was the superlative of superlatives."

It was. Did Zach think so too? "Really?"

"I wouldn't have said it if it wasn't so." He kisses me. "You may recall we had a discussion about honesty and saying only what we mean."

"Yes. I remember. We drank to it."

"But we didn't have dinner," Zach reminds me. "I can run out and rustle up some fast food before I head for home. I just have to rest for a few moments."

"You don't have to go out, Zach. We have food here. If you're hungry, I'll make you something to eat. And you're welcome to stay."

"I'm more exhausted than hungry, so thank you for the invite. I was dreading the drive home."

"You'll stay? I won't have to sleep alone?"

"Of course I'll stay. If I had my druthers, you wouldn't sleep another night alone."

Zach turns to me and looks into my eyes. He takes my hands in his and says, "I'm not only in like and in lust with you, but I've fallen in love with you, Kaitlyn. You are the first and only woman I've said those words to." He takes me into his arms and says, "I want to hold you while we sleep."

I cuddle up with Zach and dream happy dreams.

Chapter Forty-One

I hear Zach awaken and get out of bed. I think about our lovemaking last night and sigh. I shiver, reliving every incredibly wonderful moment, as I watch him dress from my prone position on my bed. He's such a hunk. Fully dressed, he sits down on the bed beside me and says, "Happy Thanksgiving, Kaity."

I sit up and say, "And to you, Zach. Happy Thanksgiving."

"Do you have plans for Thanksgiving dinner?" he asks.

"Dinner with my folks," I answer. "How about you?"

"Usually with my folks, but this year they're out of town. They went on a Thanksgiving cruise with some friends of theirs."

"Come celebrate Thanksgiving with me and my folks. I'd like you to meet them, and then we can come back here and have dessert. In my bedroom."

"You've got yourself a deal, pretty lady." He leans over to kiss me, and I put my arms around his neck. "I'll walk you out," I say and grab my robe.

We kiss at the door and Zach says, "I'll see you later, sweet girl."

~ * ~

I call Zach later that morning and ask him to pick me up at four o'clock for dinner with my folks. "They're looking forward to meeting you."

I check my messages and see that Matt emailed me:

Happy Thanksgiving, Kaity. I hope we're still friends.

I respond:

Happy Thanksgiving, Matt.

I close my phone and go into my bedroom to get dressed. I decide on a red knit slack outfit, and I'm ready to go when Zach arrives.

"Wow," he says, you're gorgeous. Red is your color," he says and leans down and kisses me.

He's wearing brown dress slacks and a silky tan dress shirt beneath his bomber jacket.

"You're pretty darn gorgeous yourself, Zach. A hunk if there ever was one. And I want to inhale you."

He slings his arm around my neck. "What we have here, I believe, is a mutual admiration society."

I laugh. "Let's go scarf down Thanksgiving dinner so we can come back here and languish over dessert."

And we are on our way to Irene and Charlie Kinney's home for dinner.

~ * ~

We arrive at my folks' home, and I introduce Zach to my mom and dad. A football game is playing on the television in the bungalow's cozy living room, and Zach gets comfortable to watch football with my dad, a senior citizen with a full head of white hair and twinkling blue eyes.

I go into the kitchen with my mom to help with the final dinner preparations. My mom is an older version of me, her once auburn hair a lovely grey, which is twisted into a knot and pinned atop her head. Like me, she's also short and slender. She almost always has a playful look about her.

We enjoy a traditional Thanksgiving dinner of turkey and stuffing and mashed potatoes and gravy, along with a few glasses of wine. We all pitch in to clear the table and clean up after dinner.

"How about dessert?" Irene asks.

Zach and I look at one another and smile.

"We've got apple or pumpkin pie," Irene says.

"Apple for me, my dear," Charlie says. "But hold the whipped cream. I want to save it for later," he says with a smile on his lips and a twinkle in his eyes.

The youthful Irene blows him a kiss.

"Thanks, Mom," I say, "but I'm stuffed."

"Thanks for a delicious meal, Mrs. Kinney," Zach says, "but same here. I couldn't eat another bite."

"Then we'll wrap up a couple of slices you can take home with you," Irene tells us.

I follow my mom into the kitchen. "No dessert, my backside," she says. "The apple did not fall far from the tree, Kaitlyn, and you're not fooling me. I see the way you two look at one another, and you're planning to have each other for dessert."

I laugh.

My mom puts a couple of pie slices in a plastic container and opens a paper sack. "I like him, Kaity. So does Dad. And the way he looks at you is the same way that Dad looks at me. I think you may finally have found love."

I think so too—hope so—but remind myself I need to be cautious. "I don't want to make another mistake."

"If this is the true love you've been searching for, your heart will be overwhelmed and burst with joy, Kaity. Trust your heart."

I hug my mother.

"Go give Dad a hug while I get your to-go bag ready," my mom tells me.

~ * ~

Ann Moran

On the drive back to my house after Thanksgiving dinner, Zach says, "I like your folks. Thanks for inviting me to dinner."

"I'm glad you came, Zach. So were my folks. They like you, too."

"Your folks are very much in love with one another. They smile at each other a lot and consistently make eye contact. And they're playful with one another, like the bit with the whipped cream. My folks would never say anything like that in front of other people. They love each other, but it's more of a passive love. Your folks' kind of love is special. Their love radiates off them and warms the room." Eyes on the road, Zach takes a quick glance at me and says, "You are fortunate, Kaity, to have a mom and dad that not only love each other but are *in love* with one another as well."

I look over at Zach. "Now that you've made me think about it, I realize you're right. I guess I've taken it for granted. Thanks for pointing it out to me."

"I have something else to tell you, Kaity. You are well aware I like being prepared. So, while you were in the kitchen with your mom, your dad and I had a good talk. It seemed the right time to ask him for your hand, and so I did. When you're ready, of course. Your dad told me I'm the only guy who asked his permission."

"My dad loves time-honored traditions," I say, "and knowing my dad the way I do, that would have made him very happy. So, what did he say?"

"He shook my hand and gave me his blessing."

I am not surprised.

~ * ~

We are back at my house and hardly in the door before we peel off our jackets and drop them to the floor. Along with the paper sack containing the pie slices, which makes a thunk on the carpeting.

Zach puts his hands on my shoulders and kisses me, then moves his hands down over my breasts. "Oh my, no bra," he says. He slides his hands under my knit top and caresses my breasts with his fingertips.

I unzip my slacks and wiggle them to the floor. "No panties either," I tell him.

We head to my bedroom and finish undressing. Both of us naked, we sit on my bed and embrace. We fall back and share a passionate kiss, and our lovemaking is sweet and completely satisfying. I kiss Zach's lips and sit up. "How about some pie?"

"I can't think of a better way to top off dessert than with another dessert," Zach says, and sits up with me. "I'll pick up the pie from the living room floor and meet you in the kitchen."

I go into the kitchen and place plates and forks on the table. Zach comes into the kitchen and removes the container from the paper sack. He says, "There's a can of whipped cream in here."

I smile to myself. "My Mom thinks of everything."

"I'll say," Zach says.

"Apple or pumpkin?"

"Just like Charlie, apple for me, my dear. But unlike Charlie, I'd like to save the pie for later and use the whipped cream now," he says, and he picks up the can of whipped cream and leads me back to my bedroom.

~ * ~

After another round of lovemaking, Zach lays beside me, and I lay my head on his chest. "We're going to have to change these sheets so we can sleep," I say, and get up to get clean sheets and blankets.

We change the bedding and then crawl into the newly made-up bed. "Will we be able to share a room in Boston?" I ask.

"Of course."

"I thought we might have to be discrete. Because of the rest of the team."

"Fuck discretion. I'm going to tell the team I fell in like with you. Scratch that." Zach turns to me and looks into my eyes. He takes my hands in his and says, "As you are aware, I'm in love with you, Kaitlyn, and I want the whole fucking world to know it."

Zach kisses me and adds, "Besides, according to what Abby tells me, we aren't fooling anybody. The team suspects, and—Abby's words—they think it's cute that we don't have a clue they're on to us."

I laugh and kiss his lips. "I'm sleepy, Zach."

"Are you telling me we're not sleeping? I thought I was asleep and having wonderful dreams," he says and turns on his side. He wraps his arms around me, and I nestle my backside into his frontside. Zach holds me close, spooning with me, and we fall into a peaceful slumber.

Chapter Forty-Two

I awaken and hear Zach in the shower. I knew he'd be in a hurry to head to the office, so I slip into a robe and go into the kitchen. I fry bacon, scramble eggs and toast bread because I want him to eat before he leaves.

He comes into the kitchen and says, "And she cooks too. I don't ever want to wake up from these wonderful dreams I'm having." He smiles and kisses me.

"Unshaven and sexy," I say and kiss him back. "I suspected you'd be anxious to get to the office, so I wanted to be sure you had a decent meal before you headed out. Sit. Would you like coffee?"

He sits. "Yes, please."

I place a dish of raspberry jam on the table and pour coffee. "Just cream, right?"

"I'm begging you. Please don't wake me."

I smile, and we both dig into our breakfasts.

When we're finished eating, Zach pulls me onto his lap. "I'm sorry I'm going to have to eat and run, Kaity, but I've got so much work to do."

I put my hands on the sides of his face and kiss him. "I know, Zach," I remind him. "I get it. Remember?"

"I begged you," he says, and I smile again.

Zach opens my robe and nuzzles his face against my breasts.

"Do I smell like whipped cream?"

"You smell like sex, and I want you," he says, and his lips pull at a nipple, and he sucks.

I feel the wet begin, and I reach down and touch him. He's hardening beneath my touch, and I ask, "Do you have time for some morning lovemaking?"

Zach strokes the side of my face with his fingertips. "I will always have time to make love to you," and he lifts me up and carries me back to bed.

~ * ~

After our lovemaking, I go back to the kitchen and clean up the breakfast dishes while Zach takes another shower. Dressed again, he comes into the kitchen and says, "These next few days are going to be brutal in terms of the work I have to get done."

We walk to the front door together, and Zach embraces me. "I'll make it up to you after the trial."

We kiss, and Zach is on his way.

~ * ~

Zach calls me after working most of the day and late into the night. "I wish you were here with me. I want to fall asleep holding you in my arms."

"Do you want me to grab an Uber and come to you?"

"Yes, but no. Thank you for the offer, Kaity, but it's much too late. I'm going to dream about holding you and kissing you and touching you and making love to you."

"What a coincidence, Zach, because that's my dream too. I'll see you in my dreams."

"Good night, Kaity, and may your dreams be as sweet as you are."

Chapter Forty-Three

Zach calls me on Saturday afternoon and tells me that he needs a break. "Would you be up for having dinner with me?"

"How about if I make you dinner?"

"I don't want you to go to any trouble."

"It won't be any trouble," I tell him. "We'll have dinner, and then you can relax for a while. Spend the night and get some sleep."

"If I spend the night, I won't get any sleep."

I laugh. "Yes, you will. I'll give you a backrub, and you'll fall right to sleep. I guarantee it. You will think you have gone to heaven."

"I already think that."

I laugh again. "I'll see you when you get here."

~ * ~

I peel and quarter potatoes and put them into the crockpot. Then I season a pot roast and put it into the pot atop the potatoes. Next, I add cream of mushroom soup. I shake in some minute pudding to thicken the gravy and turn on the pot. In a couple of hours, I'll put together a spinach salad and steam string beans. Comfort food.

Dinner is ready when Zach arrives. He kisses me and hands me a bottle of wine. "Something smells sensational in here."

I take his jacket and hang it in the hall closet. "Pot roast. I hope you're hungry."

"Hungry for you. Mostly. But the delectable aroma of the pot roast is making me salivate."

"Come into the kitchen. Dinner is ready."

Zach follows me into the kitchen, and I hand him a corkscrew. He uncorks the wine, and I add wine glasses to our place settings. Zach pours the wine after allowing it to breathe for a bit, and then we sit down and enjoy dinner.

When we finish eating, Zach says, "Thank you, Kaity. I believe that may be the most delicious meal I've ever eaten." He gets up and begins to clear the table. "You cooked; I'll clean."

"Not tonight, Zach. You've been burning the candle at both ends. Please go into the living room and get comfortable. Sit and relax. I'll join you shortly and rub your back."

I rinse off dishes and put leftovers into the fridge. I cork the remaining wine and leave it on a kitchen counter. When I finish the cleanup and go into the living room, I find Zach sound asleep in a corner of my sofa, Bocelli playing softly from my CD player, and I smile. I remove his shoes and lift his legs onto the sofa, then go into my room and get a warm blanket to cover him.

I kiss him and sit at the other end of the sofa. I could learn to love this man. As I watch him sleep, I wonder if maybe I already do. The knot in my heart continues to unravel, and I keep watch until I fall asleep.

~ * ~

I awaken when Zach shifts his legs and sits up. "Sorry, Kaity, I tried not to wake you."

"I'm glad you did. We'll be more comfortable sleeping in my bed than lying out here on the sofa all night."

We go into my room and undress, and Zach lies down on my bed. I sit on my bed and say, "It's time for your backrub."

"Not tonight, Kaity. Please just lie beside me."

I lie beside him, and Zach turns to me and begins to stroke my forehead. "Thank you for a wonderful dinner. And for letting me sleep," he says and kisses me.

I reach down and touch him and feel that he's hard. "How tired are you?"

"I will never be too tired to make love to you," he says, and his fingertips touch my breasts. He leans over and gently bites the nipple of one breast before he sucks it and then does the same to the other.

I moan softly, and Zach inserts a finger into my wetness. I see he is large and hard, and I'm sopping by the time he moves above me. He plunges his cock into me, and I cry out. He thrusts, and I raise my hips to meet his thrust. He thrusts again and pounds into me, and I keep pace with him as waves of wet surge throughout my body.

He continues to thrust and pound, and I continue to match him, a series of orgasmic waves racing through me until I can no longer hold back. "I'm going to come, Zach!" I cry out.

He says, "I'm coming with you, Kaity!" and we shudder together and climax as one.

We're both breathing heavily and working to catch our breath. I turn toward Zach and lay my head on his chest. "That was incredible," I say. "You're incredible."

"Spectacular, Kaity, because you are truly spectacular in every way," he says and kisses me.

"Are you tired?"

Zach takes me into his arms and says, "Tired? I thought I was asleep and in the midst of an incredibly spectacular dream."

And I fall asleep with a smile on my face.

Chapter Forty-Four

Zach is in the shower when I awaken. I go into the bathroom and ask him if he wants company.

He laughs and says, "I can't believe I'm going to turn you down, Kaity, but not this time. I have to go to the office and pick up the materials we need for the trial, and I have to go home and get packed for tomorrow. Can I have a shower check?"

"Of course. Would you like me to come to the office with you? Is there anything I can help you with?"

Zach turns off the water, and I hand him a towel. "I believe I'm in good shape, but you're welcome to come with me if you like, and we can stay at my place tonight."

"I'll pack and come with you. Then we can go to the airport together tomorrow."

Zach leans over to kiss me and says, "Good plan."

I rub my hands against his unshaven face and into his curly wet hair. "You sexy man. I want to gobble you up."

Zach smiles and says, "That works for me," and he kisses me again.

I pack my suitcase while Zach dries off and gets dressed. I go into my home office and pack my case summaries and reports into my briefcase. I check my email, and there's a message from Matt:

Hi Kaity, I hope you are well. I'm still working on trying to find the direction my life should take. I hope you'll bear with me. Sending love, Matt.

I close out of my email without responding and turn off my computer.

"Ready?" Zach asks.

"Set, go," I reply, and we head for downtown Chicago.

~ * ~

Zach and I stop at the office to pack the files and binders he needs for trial. It would have been more convenient to box the heavy trial bags and have them FedExed to our Boston hotel, but Zach—always the ultimate preparer and planner—prefers to keep his files at his fingertips days before a trial is scheduled to begin.

We leave the office toting the heavy bags and put them into the "frunk" of Zach's Porsche. It's a tight squeeze, but we manage to fit in both trial bags, my suitcase and both our briefcases.

"Sorry, Kaity, but we're going to have to lug all this stuff up to my condo," Zach says. "You might have to hold my suitcase on your lap on the way to the airport. Kidding," he says and laughs. "We're taking a limo to the airport, but I'm not kidding about having to lug the heavy stuff upstairs."

Zach drives out of the parking garage and asks, "Would you like to stop somewhere for lunch before we head to my place?"

"Nope, I'm good," I tell him. "I'd like to get all the stuff done we need to do so that we can relax a bit."

"I hope 'relax' is code for making love," he says, and I laugh.

~ * ~

We arrive at Zach's lakefront condo, load the heavy trial bags along with my suitcase and our briefcases into the elevator, and ride up to the thirty-third floor. Zach unlocks the door, and we carry everything into his condo. He hangs up our jackets in a closet, and I walk to look out the floor-to-ceiling windows that provide a magnificent view of Lake Michigan.

Zach stands behind me and puts his hands on my shoulders, then turns me around to face him and looks into my eyes. "I love you, Kaitlyn—he holds up a hand—please don't say anything. I've waited a long time for you, and I'm willing to wait longer, as long as it takes."

"I'm in like with you, Zach," I say. "And I'm also in lust with you, as you may have already guessed."

Zach smiles. "That's good for now," he says and kisses me. "Please make yourself at home. I'll go pack."

"I'm suddenly hungry," I say.

"There are snacks in the pantry and beer and wine, including Zinfandel, in the refrigerator, Kaity. Please help yourself."

"It's you I'm hungry for, Zach."

"I believe I've been Pinged," he says.

Zach lifts me into his arms and carries me into his bedroom.

~ * ~

We undress each other and make sweet passionate love. I'm flushed and breathless in its aftermath, and Zach pulls me into his arms. He kisses and hugs me, and says, "I'm deeply in love with you, Kaity, and I love you with everything I've got, my entire being—heart and soul, mind and body."

I know I have to say something, but I'm so afraid of making another mistake. I look into his eyes and say, "And I may be on my way to falling in love with you, Zach. Thank you for understanding I may not have gotten all the way there yet."

"I'm hoping to make you mine, Kaitlyn. I've sown my wild oats, so to speak, and I pledge on all that I am to do all that I can to make you happy. I intend to propose to you, but I'll wait until it feels right for you," Zach tells me, then gets out of bed and goes to get his suitcase.

Zach is an amazing man, who already makes me truly happy. I feel certain I'm on my way to falling in love with him. I'm almost there, and the knot in my heart is nearly undone.

~ * ~

Zach finishes packing and then works for a while, while I run out to pick up cheeseburgers for dinner. We eat and turn in early.

We undress and climb into bed together. We spoon, and Zach kisses the back of my neck. It takes hardly a moment before he's hard, his erection pressed into my backside, and I feel a whole lot of wet gathering between my legs.

"You are so beautiful," he says and kisses me long and deep. "Turn over. I'm going to put my cock into you, and I want you to watch me do it."

I turn onto my back. I watch as Zach inserts the tip of his dick into my opening, and I feel a wave of wet rush through me. He lowers his mouth to my breasts and his tongue licks my nipples. His lips tug at a nipple and his teeth nip a bit. Then his lips suck my nipple into his mouth. He sucks soft and deep and continues his ministrations on my other breast. Tug, nip, suck and he repeats it over and over again.

I'm writhing with wet, and Zach pushes his dick a little further into me. "Tell me what you want, Kaity."

"I want you to make love to me," I say, and watch as he plunges his large cock all the way into me and begins to pump, softly and gently. "Faster, Zach!"

"What would you like me to do faster, Kaity?"

"Fuck me faster!"

"I'm going to fuck you faster and harder than you've ever been fucked before," and Zach does exactly what he says he would do. He fucks me harder and faster than I've ever been fucked, and waves of orgasm race through my body. I moan aloud as he pushes and pounds and plunges, over and over, harder and faster, and his cock is touching and plunging into places I didn't know I had. I'm on fire! The pounding he's giving me is going to tear me apart. I'll heal! And a succession of euphoric waves course through my body, and my climax is one of the most amazing I've ever experienced.

Zach climaxes with me, and he holds me in his arms. He strokes my brow and says, "I will always do whatever I can to give you the most pleasure in love and in life. I want to know whatever your heart desires. Whatever your body desires as well. Okay?"

I look up at Zach and say, "If I'm asleep and dreaming, please don't wake me."

He smiles at me, and we kiss and fall asleep in one another's arms.

Chapter Forty-Five

After awakening the next morning, Zach and I get into the shower together. It's a large shower with a shower bench. The bench is marble-tiled and is set beneath a pair of toiletry niches, which take a back seat to the vivid blue tiles that are inset in the adjacent wall. In that way, the solid marble bench seat distinguishes itself from the rest of the tiled backdrop.

We lather up our hands and soap each other up as the water pelts down on us. Zach's dick is fully erect, and I feel the wet gathering between my legs. He sits down on the bench and pulls me to him. I'm sopping wet when I ease myself onto his erection, and Zach plunges up and into me. I cry out, and he begins to pump and pound, and I pump and pound with him, lifting my hips up and down as I ride his thick cock. An orgasm rushes through me, and I climax as Zach shivers and shudders, and I fall into his arms.

We kiss and Zach says, "That was an amazing way to start the day, Kaity," and he kisses me again.

We clean ourselves, rinse off, and step out of the shower. We towel each other dry with large fluffy bath towels, and dress in comfy jeans and sweaters.

~ * ~

Zach and I put on our jackets, and we're ready to go. We head down to the condo lobby, lugging trial bags, rolling suitcases, carrying briefcases and Zach's garment bag. Our limo has arrived, and the driver is standing outside the limo. He helps Zach load the heavy trial bags and the rest of the luggage into the trunk of the large automobile. When we're seat-belted inside, the driver pulls away from the curb and heads to O'Hare Airport.

Zach has his arm around my shoulders, and I rest my head against his chest. We both close our eyes and catch a quick nap on the way to the airport.

~ * ~

We arrive at the United Airlines terminal, and our limo driver unloads our luggage and trial bags from the trunk. He hands them off to a skycap, who tags each piece at the curb. Zach hands generous gratuities to both the driver and the skycap, and we enter the large airport concourse through the automatic doors.

We check in and get our boarding passes. In order to get to our gate, we make our way through United's series of moving walkways that connect beneath the eight-hundred-foot rainbow of neon tubes that light up and reflect off overhead mirrors.

The rest of the trial team has already arrived. They are sitting in seats in the gate area, the three associates—Jason Whitely, Stefanie Jones and Gregory Norris—sitting on one side and Abby, Michael Cole and Maria Shue sitting on the other side.

The associates immediately rise to greet Zach, and Abby jumps up to give me a hug. Michael, my paralegal counterpart, waves a "hello" and Maria Shue, the other secretary, smiles and waves as well.

I sit down beside Abby and squeeze her hand, getting another chance to admire her magnificent engagement ring.

Zach stands in the midst of the team. I look at him, and my heart is filled with a full and overflowing warmth, a phenomenal feeling of joy I've not before fully experienced. My heart hammers as I am overwhelmed with a love more extraordinary than I've ever known. And I know. My heart knows, and I trust my heart. I have no doubt about it. I finally realize I'm in love with Zach, and my heart thunders, and the knotty ache in my heart shatters and falls to pieces.

"Okay, team," Zach says. "I've got a couple of things I'd like to tell you so there's no gossiping or snickering behind our backs," and he motions for me to come and stand beside him. "As some of you may know, Kaity and I have known each other for more than twenty years. I finally worked up the nerve to ask her out, and we're dating." Zach puts an arm around my shoulders and kisses the top of my head. "She's short, but she's sweet."

And the team laughs.

"She's going to sit up front with me and share my suite at the hotel."

The trial team rise as one and applauds.

The team's applause gets the attention of other passengers in the gate area, as well as the gate agents at the counter and the flight attendant at the entrance to the airline's jetway. All eyes are now on me and Zach.

I stand on the tips of my toes and whisper into Zach's ear, "I'm in love with you, Zach."

"Excuse us for just a moment, team," Zach says. He turns to face me, puts his hands on my shoulders, and whispers to me, "You're what?"

I nod my head vigorously.

"You're certain?"

I smile up at him. "Absolutely. I'm deeply in love with you, Zach, and it's beyond belief that it's taken me so long to realize that you're the man I want to spend the rest of my life with."

Zach embraces me and holds me tight. "If I'm asleep and dreaming, please don't wake me."

I laugh again. "You're wide awake, Zach. I'm the one who's been asleep, and it's about time I woke up. I'm going to have to get a new name plate."

"You'll take my name?"

"Kaitlyn Eberle. It has a nice ring to it."

"Speaking of a nice ring," Zach says and waves Abby over. Abby slips off her ring and hands it to Zach. I'm astounded.

Zach takes both of my hands in his and gets down on one knee. "Kaitlyn Kinney, will you do me the honor of becoming my wife?"

I throw my arms around his neck and shout, "Yes! Yes, yes, yes!"

Zach slips the ring onto my finger, and I feel the way I imagine Cinderella must have felt when she put her foot into the glass slipper. Zach takes me into his arms. He lifts me up and spins me around, and the applause in the gate area is deafening.

~ * ~

Enroute to Boston, Zach and I sit side by side. I keep looking at my ring, and I'm amazed he recruited Abby to help him have the perfect ring available to place on my finger when I was ready to accept his proposal. I shake my head, wondering why I'm surprised when I'm fully aware that the man of my dreams is always prepared.

Zach has plenty of legroom in Row One, and his long legs are stretched out before him. I look at him and see that his eyes are closed. Apparently sensing me looking at him, he says, "Just because my eyes are closed doesn't mean I'm sleeping."

I check my email and see that Matt has written:

Hi Kaity, I still don't know what direction I'm headed, but I'm confident I will get to wherever I'm destined to go if you would be willing to make the journey with me. I miss you so fucking much—yes, pun intended! —and I was thinking we could get reacquainted at LN1. I want us to share our lives and our hearts and to grow old together. What say you? Sending love, Matt.

I look at Zach again. Sensing my eyes on him again, he says, "What?"

"I love you, Zach. That's what."

Zach opens his eyes and smiles. "Promise me I'm not dreaming, and that you'll be mine forever."

I look at Matt's email again and click Delete. I close my phone and lean over to lay my head on Zach's chest. I look up at him lovingly and say, "I promise."

Zach pulls me into his arms and leans down to kiss me. And all is right with the world.

About the Author

Ann Moran has been a legal secretary for many years and has been employed in large law firms in Chicago, San Francisco and Carson City. She has been fortunate to have worked for and with some of the smartest people on the planet, and her coworkers are more like family than friends. She is a voracious reader and loves to write. She also loves music and baseball, especially the Chicago Cubs. *The Harder They Fall* was her first novel, and *Lust & Found* is her latest effort.

VISIT OUR WEBSITE

FOR THE FULL INVENTORY

OF QUALITY BOOKS:

http://www.roguephoenixpress.com

Rogue Phoenix Press

Representing Excellence in Publishing

Quality trade paperbacks and downloads

in multiple formats,

in genres ranging from historical to contemporary romance, mystery and science fiction.

Visit the website then bookmark it.

We add new titles each month!

www.ingramcontent.com/pod-product-compliance
Lightning Source LLC
Chambersburg PA
CBHW070329130626
46556CB00007B/2780